MW01527585

Tales from the Peanut Roaster

"Grandpa's memories of the two-foot gauge railroad in Monson, Maine."

d. g. bearden

Cover Painting by Raymond L. Clark
Used with permission from
Wayne and Estella Bennett

Tales from the Peanut Roaster

A fictitious narrative of

THE MONSON RAILROAD

based on true stories from the

Piscataquis Observer

and the archives of the

Monson Historical Society

d. g. bearden

DEDICATION

To Vangi DeMaster

Author, Educator, Playwright, Director

and Friend

who many years ago encouraged me to step out of my comfort zone and try something new.

Copyright 2021
By
Dale G. Bearden

ISBN 9798730349285
Library of Congress Number 1-10304027391

This is a work of fiction, any resemblance to people living or dead, except those recorded in the newspaper articles sighted herein, is unintentional, and is purely accidental.

Table of Contents

FORWARD vii

one   a beginning   1
two   two storms   7
three   butterflies   17
four   moose horns   25
five   community   39
six   narrow escape   49
seven   never give up   57
eight   fire & wind   63
nine   strange cargo   71
ten   truth or consequences   83
eleven   baked beans   89
twelve   mysteries   99
thirteen   difficult railroading   105
fourteen   troubled narrow gauge   113
fifteen   changes   121
sixteen   chores   129
seventeen   joey's back   135
eighteen   last whistle   141
nineteen   proved its worth   151
twenty   ripples   157
acknowledgments   165
references   166

Cecil Johnson, Gus Johnson, Harold Morrill, Paul Jackson, Elwin French, Albin Johnson

Foreword

The Monson Railroad started construction in 1883 and was dissolved in 1943. It was six miles long and ran on rails a mere 24 inches apart; the locomotives were small, so small that the engineer and fireman could not stand straight up in the cab. The railroad's main purpose was to haul slate from the quarries in Monson, Maine to a Junction with the standard gauge Bangor and Aroostook Railroad near Abbot. It was often called the "two by six" because of its track gauge and six mile length. The locomotives ran forward to the Junction and backwards back to Monson Village, they were never turned around.

Because of their diminutive size and their squeaky whistles, when compared to a standard gauge locomotive, the little Vulcan Forney Locomotives were affectionately called "Peanut Roasters"

This little narrow gauge railroad was the main artery for the small village of Monson, Maine. For over 60 years, it served as Monson's major year around connection with the outside world. Its challenges were many and its unspoken heroes were plenty. Until a world war and a decline in the slate business closed it down, the railroad prevailed through all kinds of weather, a worldwide flu pandemic and the great depression. Today only two locomotives and two buildings survive.

I've never lived in Maine; the Monson Railroad was dismantled and scrapped five years before I was born, but I have a passion for the little railroad that started when I was a guest engineer on restored locomotive Monson #4. For nearly 20 years I have been researching and studying the Monson Railroad.

After visiting Monson and making many friends, it is my desire to preserve not only the railroad's history, but some of the history of the folks that make up the village of Monson, Maine.

This, then, is a fictionalized, historical narrative loosely based on nearly 60 years of newspaper articles and letters taken (in no particular order) from the Monson Historical Society Archives and The Piscataquis Observer.

x

a beginning

I don't know how your mind works, but my mind seems to work backwards. The older I get the more I have to think about where I am and then back track to where I want to be.

I suppose I should back up and tell you what's going on, before you can understand what I'm even talking about.

But before I do, I guess I should tell you a little bit about myself. I was born in August of 1928; my name is Billy McCollum, and I lived in Bangor, Maine and spent most of my growing up years between there and Monson, Maine. My mom's mom and dad Clarence and Ruby White lived in Monson. I was fifteen years old in the winter of 1943, when the rails were pulled up and Monson was no more. The village is still here, but the railroad's gone.

My grandpa, Clarence White, was a section man on the Monson when I was born. He was a solid man of above average height; he had thick dark hair that he parted on the right. He was missing the first finger on his left hand. He had lost it in an accident when he was a kid back on the farm. He left the farm when he was 17 and went to work in the quarries.

Monson section crew and hand car

Right away he showed an aptitude for mechanical things and he had a special interest in the little narrow-gauge train. If he saw any chance to help out with the railroad, he would. Sometimes he'd be walking on his way home from the quarry and stop to help to put a car back on the rails or hop on board as an extra brakeman when he had the chance.

Granny White was a little on the heavy side, but tall, at least 5'7", and had long gray hair that came down almost to her waist. She kept it in a bun on the back of her head; she said that she had never cut it because the Bible said that a woman's hair was her crowning glory. She had really pretty hazel eyes that seemed to see everything I was gonna' do before I even did it. Often times she'd let me go

Granny and Grandpa

3

ahead and learn from my mistakes, but she'd never let me go so far as to hurt myself.

Sometimes in my mind I can still hear her saying "Billy Gene, you come here and let me see what kind of "truck" you've got in your pockets." I don't know why she called it "truck"; maybe it was because she could never tell what I was hauling around in my overall pockets. She got pretty used to finding rocks, and worms, and pieces of wire or string or bent nails, I think the only time I surprised her was when she pulled out a live frog. That startled her so much I was afraid she might croak —- the frog not Granny.

Startled me and the frog too; I had to really scramble to catch it again after she dropped it. Grandpa gave me a little talking to that time, so I thought twice about keeping that little garter snake I'd caught.

Her and Grandpa White lived a hard life, often times sustained by their quiet faith in the Lord. Working in the quarries was hard, dangerous work, and many men lost limbs or their lives. They counted it a blessing when Grandpa got hired on the railroad.

He took Nathan Huff's place, and it was a big pair shoes to fill. Nathan had been with the Monson Railroad as a Section hand since its beginning in 1883, and his knowledge of track work and repair work was first class. Nathan retired on May 9, 1910; my Grandpa hired on the railroad that same day.

Grandpa worked for the railroad for over 30 years, and Granny White kept every newspaper article, ticket stub and scrap of paper about the railroad she could get her hands on. I remember two big books always lying on the bureau in the front room, the Holy Bible and Granny's scrap book. Both of them looked well read.

They lived just east of Main Street on Chapin Ave. within a couple hundred yards of the station. The track curved across Chapin Ave. just before it got their house, I can remember standing in the front yard waving to the engineers as the train (when) by.

Guess I haven't really told you a lot about me, now have I? Well, suffice it to say that I'm older now; matter of fact, I'm older than my Grandpa and Granny White were when they went to that meeting in the air. Hattie and I got married in 1947 and now we're just a year short of the new Millennium.

Today we live about as far from Maine as one can and still be on the Canadian border. Northwest Washington is our home now; it's very similar to Maine, except we have a lot less snow.

As I reminisce about Monson and the railroad, I sometimes forget that the road was only six miles long, eight if you include the yard tracks at the quarries. For a kid in the 1930's, it could have been a 100 miles. When I think about all stories I heard from my Grandpa, to me it was the most important railroad in the country.

two storms

W ell, it all started on a late winter afternoon in early March, cold enough for us old people to have a fire in the wood stove, but not cold enough to snow.   The sky was full of those low, rolling, grayish-black clouds, and it wouldn't be long till dark. The rain and wind coming in gusts across the lake were strong enough to beat against the windowpanes and rattle the shutters; at least it would have rattled 'em if we had any. But that's another tale.

I'd put in a pretty good day and managed to mostly stay dry. Can't say the same thing about staying warm though; those winds across the water sure can blow cold. It don't matter which direction it comes from, they're always strong. I guess you could say we've got four strong winds.

Well, this close to Canada they ought to be strong coming down through those river valleys; guess some things just don't change.

Anyway, I'd been working on the railroad all day and me and the dog had just come in from filling up the wood box. As I was kicking my boots off by the door, I asked her what was for dinner. I mean I asked my wife, not the dog.

Hattie had the old black and white cat, LC (Elsie) on her lap and her book open in front of her. They were looking pretty comfortable, sitting in the recliner by the fire. She said she was C.O.L., and that if I was in a hurry, I was on my own for dinner.

"Well," I said, "If you're cold I'll put some more wood on the fire."

She said, "I'm not cold, I'm C period, O period, L period: Cat On Lap, and you can just as well wait until LC gets up or fix your own dinner."

Well, I wasn't that hungry besides the dog won't eat my cooking either.

We, Hattie and I, had been married over fifty years, and you'd think that as along as we've been together, I'd have heard every one of her smart remarks, but she still managed to toss one my way ever' now and then. She sure knows how to keep things interesting.

About that time there was loud bang and crash against the wall, the dog and the cat both took off toward the back of the house.

A voice yelled out, "Hi Grandma, hi Grandpa!" It was the oldest grandson Joey, followed by our oldest daughter, his mom. They came dripping in the front door and threw their coats into pile on the

8

entry bench; guess that was easier than hanging them up on the hooks above the bench.

I meant to say, "Followed by our first daughter". Nancy (We often called her Nan) hates to be called the oldest kid, even though she is.

Well, that certainly helped relieve Hattie of her C.O.L. condition, but it didn't help my hunger any.

Her and Nan began a rather animated mile-a-minute conversation about kids and grandkids and school and sewing and art and I can't remember what else. Anyway, they had succeeded in distracting me from my hunger.

As soon as one of 'em came up for air, Joey jumped into the breach of silence and said, "Ya been working on the railroad again today, Grandpa?"

I said, "Now what do you think? I'm sure not going outside in this kind of weather. Of course, I've been working on the railroad, almost all the live long day."

Then he said, "Can I see what's new?"

So, me and him, sensing our way out, headed to the railroad room. Oh, I forgot to mention, it's a model railroad layout of the Monson Railroad that used to be in Monson, Maine. My friend Karl and me are building it, and it fills the whole room.

The dog didn't seem too interested in the girl's conversation either, so she followed us.

I turned on the lights and powered up the railroad and Joey picked up the throttle and started backing old Number 3 down to the quarry for a load of slate. He was a smart kid, just turned 10 years old and a quick learner. He was already getting that tall, solid look than ran in the family; I knew he'd be a good-looking man.

He said "Grandpa, tell me another story about the Monson, you know from when you were a kid."

Now, that boy don't forget anything, except maybe his schoolwork and other important things. On one of his visits, I'd been in one of my thinking —about—things—I—forgot—I—knew moods and was remembering a story my grandpa White had told me.

You know what I mean, like you're driving down the road in the fall and the leaves are all off the trees and you are seeing things that you forgot were there. Anyway, I'd made the mistake of telling him a story that my Grandpa White told me, and now he expects me to remember one every time he comes over.

Like I told you before, Grandpa White worked on the Monson more than 30 years, and Granny White had been saving newspaper articles about Monson Village and the railroad and other stuff since before Grandpa was hired. Even with a good railroad job, things were pretty tough for Granny and Grandpa White.

Granny had a few chickens and a garden in the back yard, that she called her "Truck Farm". She worked as hard farming and cooking and cleaning and sewing as Grandpa did on the railroad. When Sunday afternoons came around and things were cleaned up after dinner, she finally had time to scrapbook a little and sometimes I'd help.

But my best memories of my Granny White were how she could cook and oh, my, how she could make chicken and dumplings.

Say that reminds me,

"Hey Joey" I said, "Have you had your supper yet?"

"Not yet, Grandpa, but I could eat a horse or something."

He probably could, you know how growing boys are. Anyway I said: "Let's go see what Grandma's got for supper and I'll tell you about the big storm of Thursday, February 26, 1920 while we eat."

Now, I remember what I was getting ready to talk about in the beginning. It was that big snowstorm of Thursday, February 26, 1920. Told you sometimes I sort have to back into things. Now, I'm sure you sometimes think about when you were young and get to marveling about some of things you heard, don't you?

Well, that storm must have been something! Granny White had saved two articles about that storm, one about the Monson, and one about how the whole state of Maine was impacted.

Snow bound

About that time, Nancy yelled from the door of the railroad room (that girl don't do anything quietly) ,"Come on Joe we've got to go home so I can fix supper for the family."

Joey yelled back (guess it runs in the family) "Ah Ma, Grandpa was just getting ready to tell me the story of the big snowstorm in February 1920."

She said "Joey, your Grandpa wasn't even born in 1920".

To which I replied "what's that got to do with it? You can stay with me Joe; I'll take you home later if the rain lets up.",

Nan said "Is that alright with you, Mom?" I had my mind made up so I answered for Mom and Joey stayed for dinner. As a matter of fact, he stayed all night. Of course, we had all forgotten that was why Nancy brought him over in the first place.

Hattie set the plates on the table and dished up the spaghetti and meat balls, and the three of us held hands asked the blessing. Joey dove into his supper like he had not eaten in a week.

"Well," I began, "that Thursday started out pretty mild, but by mid-morning, the wind was picking up and the sky was getting dark. When the men went to work at the quarries there was very little snow on the ground; still it was snowing a bit."

"By nighttime it was something fierce, the wind howling, and snow so thick you could hardly see to walk."

Joey interrupted and said, "Like it's doing outside, Grandpa?"

What? I peeked out the window and sure enough, it looked like we were going have a white lawn by morning. So I said "Yeah, just like it's doing outside, only worse. Anyway, Joe, try not to interrupt me or I'll forget where I was at. Now the old timers claimed it was the worst storm for many years. The storm was so bad that one man, at least, considered it too severe to try to get home, and he stayed all night in the boiler house. Guess he was plenty warm, might have got a little hungry though."

"That morning, before noon, the train with both locomotives attached, had headed off to the Junction. Before 12 midday, the train started backing its way back to Monson. When it reached Day's Crossing the snow was so deep that the train stalled and remained there for more than 24hours."

"The mail and passengers were brought to the village by sleds and teams of horses. That Friday, the next morning, fifty men from the Monson Slate Quarry started shoveling the snow at the station.

They shoveled every inch of the track from Monson to the stalled train, reaching it just before dark."

"Saturday, a large crew of men shoveled the three miles to number 18 quarry."

"How far was it to Day's Crossing, Grandpa?"

"About four-and-a-half or five miles I reckon. Now, Joe, remember…"

Shaking his head, he said "Sorry, Grandpa, but this is an exciting story"

"Okay, well, the next day, I mean Friday after the tracks were cleared, the Railroad resumed service. The snow was over four feet deep and it took both engines to push the snowplow to the Junction. They got through about noon and started the return trip with the mail that afternoon. They finally arrived back in Monson about five o'clock.

The newspaper on the fourth of March, reported that the last snow and blow was a very expensive one for the railroad, especially when coupled with the earlier storms."

"I guess it cost a lot to pay fifty men to shovel snow for a whole day." Joey said, told you he was a smart kid.

Grandma reminded me to hush and eat my supper before it got any colder. Joey wanted seconds, I was still eating my first, so we got down

15

to business and finished the story and supper at the same time.

Joey helped with the supper dishes, and I was still thinking about that big snow storm; I was feeling like I was missing something. I dug Granny White's scrapbook out from the bottom of the book case, and started flipping through it.

Good thing she had kept things in pretty much chronological order, I easily found the other article from the 'Piscataquis Observer' dated May 26, 1920, and found what I was missing.

The headline stated:

THE HEAVIEST STORM OF THE WINTER

It reported that the *"fall of snow was accompanied by high winds which packed the snow drifts so solidly the usual method of plowing out the sidewalks had to be abandoned, and practically all of the towns had to be shoveled before the plows could get through."*

It said that it was a good thing that the storm had been a short one; otherwise it would have been blizzard conditions and possibly deaths would have ensued. The Maine Central train for Newport was 25 hours late, the B & A train from Greenville didn't arrived until 10am Friday, and even the rural mail carriers were unable to deliver the mail until Saturday.

Chapter Three

butterflies in the stomach

Seems I was right! We definitely had a white lawn the next morning. As a matter of fact, if we'd had another three-and-half feet or so, we'd have rivaled that snow of 1920. It was deep enough that I that I decided I'd slip on a pair of shoes instead of wearing my house slippers out to load the wood box and pick up the newspaper.

When Joe got up I was sitting at the table, glancing through the paper and sipping on my coffee. LC and the dog were both curled up by the wood stove.

Hattie asked us what we wanted for breakfast, and before Joe could answer; I said "Why don't you fry up some those fresh butterflies I caught this morning, Grandma?"

Grandma said, "That's a great idea; it'll be quick and easy and you boys can get outside and finish splitting that load of wood before the snow gets any deeper."

Joey was shaking his head and I asked him what was wrong. "I don't think I like butterflies."

"Well, Joe, you ever ate one?" His Grandma asked "No, then you better try one before you decide." and she turned back to the stove.

"You know, Joe, an early morning like today is the best time to hunt butterflies, and the best time to eat'em is when they are warm. It's sort of like eating crow; it best to eat crow while it's still warm." I told him.

Joey was looking at me like I was nuts and he cried "We're not gonna have crow for lunch, are we?"

I said,"I certainly hope not!" Just then Hatti set our plates down in front of us, and before I could say grace Joey said "This looks like French toast that's just shaped like a butterfly."

Hatti grinned and said, "Well what do you know. Just like my granny made for me, a piece of bread cut on a diagonal and two strips of bacon. The two slices of bread make the wings and the bacon is the body."

We bowed our heads, and gave thanks, and then I passed him the syrup. It was a good thing my "butterfly hunt" was successful; that boy almost ate the whole limit.

I put on my boots and Joey and me grabbed our gloves and hats and headed out the back door. Naturally, the dog followed us. The temperature wasn't very warm, and it was getting colder by degrees, but we kept plenty warm splitting and stacking wood. The snow was still falling and the flakes were getting bigger, the wind was getting weaker. The dog went to work sniffing around the woodshed.

It must have taken all of 15-minutes before Joey was losing interest in the work and starting to complain.

"Joe" I said, "do you ever think about how good we've got it? Think about those 50 men shoveling through four feet of snow for five miles, here we are, with a power splitter and warm house 50 feet away. And you're whining and I'm already tired. Anyway, when we get done with our chores, I've a little railroad project that I need help on.

So, we finished the wood, and dumped the ashes and the trash and the three of us, me, Joey and the dog, moved into the railroad room to warm up. Joe wanted to run the trains some more, but we had to do a little clean up first.

I'd sorta got in the habit of making a big mess when I was working on the railroad, then leaving it until I couldn't stand it, or Karl was coming out, which ever came first. Since Joey was here, I put him to work cleaning up under the railroad.

That's an odd way to say something isn't it; I mean how can you be "up" and "under" something at the same time. I don't know what that has to do with the story; it just sort of popped into my mind.

Anyway, Karl was coming out tomorrow to work in the railroad. Surely you can remember Karl; he's helping build the railroad. He is my best friend and coconspirator. He liked to have the place clean when he came to work; that way he could make his own mess. We won't talk about who cleans up that mess.

Finally, things were in rather good shape so I told Joey he could run the train until his mom came to pick him up.

Now, I'm sure you remember his mom interrupting us last night, or us getting hungry or something. Anyway, I turned on the power and old Number 3 crashed right into a flat car that was parked on a siding by the mill and knocked the mill building right off its foundation. Seems somebody forgot to do something.

Joey got excited and started apologizing, and I started laughing.

He wondered what I was laughing at, and I told him that he had just done in miniature something that I had been told really did happen.

"Come on Joey; let's go get a cup of hot chocolate and I'll tell you the story; besides it almost time for your mom to show up anyway. That is if she don't get stuck"

As we were starting out the door, I asked him "Did you turn the throttle off this time?"

He said he "wasn't going to forget that ever again, 'cause that crash really scared me." It didn't do the mill building any good either, but nobody got hurt and I could fix the building.

While Hatti was making the hot chocolate, I went over to get my Granny White's old scrap book again. I was sipping my chocolate, wishing it was coffee, and thumbing thru the scrap book. I was getting so wrapped up in reading the old ads and stories I almost forgot which story I was going tell Joey.

I showed him an ad for a "SIMPLEX" bed warmer, the ad read:

"Our forefathers used the bothersome old 'warming pans' to take the chill out of their beds before retiring.

Our fathers used the rubber hot water bottles.

We are more fortunate today, for we have electricity and the Simplex Electric Heating Pad safe, sure and simple."

Well, that was a mistake, because I had to explain what a warming pan was, and that hot water bottles were not the same as water balloons, even though they were both made of rubber. I was having a hard time convincing him. Then Grandma brought out an old water bottle that we kept around for some strange reason and showed him what one looked like.

Then he wanted to know why we kept it if we weren't going to use it to warm the bed with.

So, I dug the hole deeper when I said, "Old people sometimes have a "special" use for it."

When he insisted on knowing what that "special" use was, I handed the ball off to the Grandma, and kept looking for the article that I thought I remembered.

Finally, I found the article I was looking for; it was from Monday October 9, 1916. Actually, I found two interesting articles from that day. I skimmed the articles, trying to figure out how I could make them sound exciting, then I decided that the man who was there could tell the story better than me.

Hattie was still trying to not answer the question about the hot water bottle, when I came to her rescue and said, "Hey, Joey, listen to this, I want to read you the actual article from 1916." I had his attention so I began reading:

"Considerable excitement was caused Friday at the Monson Maine Slate when a car load of crated slate was driven through the side of the Mill."

"Does that remind you of anything?" I asked. He gave me a sheepish look and forgot about the hot water bottle. So I continued reading the article:

"The accident was caused by the brakes not holding the two heavy car loads of coal which were being taken into the quarry. The grade is very steep and when the cars struck the car loaded with slate they drove it through the mill. Engineer Carlberg and Fireman Ackerson, after doing all they could, jumped from the engine and escaped injury. Luckily no one was hurt when the car came through."

"See, Joe, you really did manage to do in miniature what the real railroad did." And we both started to laugh. His grandma joined us, but I don't think she knew why we were laughing so hard.

Finally we settled down, and I read the other article to Joe and Hattie.

"October 9, 1916: Work on the new State road around Doughty hill is nearing completion. The first automobile to pass over this new piece of

road was a Dort owned and driven by A.S. Knight. On Thursday afternoon Mr. and Mrs. Knight, Superintendent of the work and Mrs. Hill and Engineer Greenwood went over the new road, covering the distance in four and one-half minutes. It is understood that the road will not be opened to the public this fall as the surfacing is yet to be put on."

Before Joe could ask, I told him that a Dort was a car that had a Lycoming engine in it. That just about opened another can of worms when he wanted to know what a Lycoming was.

About that time, Nanr showed up, and things got loud for a bit. Loud or not, she's a joy.

After they left, me and Hattie sat down and looked at each other with silly grins on our faces and started chuckling about old people and hot water bottles and their uses.

Chapter four

moose horns

As I stood up to put Granny White's scrapbook away, I caught a glimmer of snow falling outside the window. I'd already had a pretty busy day for an old boy my age, so I poured myself that cup of coffee I'd been wishing for and sat back down and opened the book back up. Besides, there's no way Karl would show up on a snowy day.

If it kept on snowing and blowing, I might end up having to shovel my way to the woodshed, but I might as well finish my coffee and see how things piled up.

I ran across an article that I remembered helping Granny White cut out of the paper and put in her scrap book, and it wasn't long until I had cast my memory back there to my first visit to Grandpa and Granny White's house in Monson. In my mind I relived every moment of that visit.

I must have been about five or six, so it was around 1933 or 1934. (I suspect I'd been here before, but this was the first visit I could recall). I guess in the early 30's, during the depression, it didn't matter if you lived in small town or a big city; times were hard. We were lucky cause my dad still had a job with Coles Transportation down in Bangor, even though his pay was cut. And Grandpa was still hanging on with the railroad, although I learned later that the railroad was barely hanging on itself.

For me, all I could think about was going to see Grandpa and Granny and being able to get up close to the train. I didn't know or care about how blessed we were, at least not until I got a little older. By the time I was eleven or twelve I was doing whatever I could to earn a little money and help out the family. I'd clean horse stalls, split wood, shovel snow; I tried my hand at any job I could beg or was offered. Sometimes, Mr. Morrill would let me sweep the station platform, and he'd pay me a nickel. Of course, it wasn't like I really had a choice, we all had to pitch in to make it.

But I'm drifting off course a bit.

It was getting close to time for my little brother or sister to be born, so Dad brought me up to Granny's to stay for a while. I think he mostly wanted to keep me out of Mom's hair. At the time I don't think I really cottoned to the idea of having a little brother or sister, but the whole matter seemed to be out of my hands anyway.

My little brother Vernon had arrived by the time I went back to Bangor after that visit.

That Sunday morning early, my mom and dad were off back home to Bangor. Dad had to work the next day, and in those days, it was almost a full day drive to get from Monson to Bangor. It was a clear spring morning, warm, with just a hint of a breeze. It was only a short walk to the Baptist Church in town, so me and Grandpa and Granny headed off to church.

I remember feeling pretty grown up going to church without my mom and dad, and I didn't put up any fuss at all. Funny, I don't remember walking home; maybe that's why Granny woke me up to eat Sunday dinner. I realized latter that Grandpa had carried me most of the way home.

But you can be sure I was wide awake when Granny set a plate of chicken and dumplings in front of me. After a boy's size serving of Granny's peach cobbler, I helped dry the silverware. I would've done more but experience had taught Granny that I didn't do a very good job on the big stuff, and she couldn't afford for me to keep dropping and breaking plates.

After dinner Grandpa was telling me about being at work a week or so before I came up. He said it was the last snow they'd had, and he had been told to ride to the junction to help unload slate. He told me even though the little cab on the Forney was crowded with four men inside, it was warm, and then the train had run out of coal and it wasn't so warm anymore.

I knew he was pulling my leg, 'cause trains don't run out of coal. My daddy's Model T had run out of gas a time or two. But I just couldn't believe a locomotive could run out of coal.

Grandpa said, "What do you think that article Granny's cutting out of the paper says?" as he pulled the paper out of Granny's grasp and handed it to me and pointed to where she had started to cut. "Read that."

I just shook my head and said "Aw Pa, you know I can't read that, I'm only almost six."

He handed the paper back to Granny and said, "Read it to him Granny"

So she did:

"Monson Railroad proves that it gets through today as it did in the early days when there were real winters (like this one.) It has been their custom to take coal at the Junction and that would last until they returned, and that was what they did Friday. But Friday night it was necessary to run down to Monson Maine Slate quarry, and they had a break down that made it necessary to draw the fire and make repairs. That was done and Saturday

after several hours of high wind they started for Monson Junction with the engine and snowplow and a very small supply of coal."

Then Grandpa said, "Hold on a minute there, Granny," He could tell by looking, that Granny had all of my attention. Then he turned to me, "What do you think is about to happen Billy?"

"I don't know, Pa." I always called him "Pa" and Granny "Granny"

Grandma said, "Leave the boy alone Clarence" and went back to reading:

"About halfway down they ran out of coal and had to stop."

"AH HA!" Grandpa exclaimed!

"CLARENCE!"

"Sorry, Ma."

I was practically in shock "But what did they do Pa?"

Granny continued, "Let's see; where was I? Oh, okay, got it."

About halfway down they ran out of coal and had to stop, but that didn't bother much, they went to a farmhouse, borrowed a buck saw and were soon sawing wood to get up steam and after a short delay plowed through to the Junction where they took on a full tender of coal and with mail and express and returned to Monson. Lots of people laugh at the little narrow gauge, but she gets there just the same, even though the drifts are piled high."

"So what do you think now, son?"

"Gosh, Pa, I'm gonna' to tell my daddy; he won't believe it."

Granny laid the paper down and Grandpa picked it up and read it silently for a bit. Then he sighed, "The paper says the past week has been a real tough one in this section. Says the big snow plow went down early Saturday morning but could not get back to Greenville. All they could do was plow back and forth from Monson Village to the Moose horns."

"What's the moose horns, Pa?" "Just what it sounds like, horns from a dead moose"

"Clarence, you tell the boy the truth."

"Well that is truth; at least it's part of it. You see, Billy, way back in 1817 a smart man named Joseph Bearce from Hebron, put a pair of moose horns way up high on a pole so folks could tell where the trail forked even in deep snow, like we got this year. When the horns got too old and start to fall off, some other hunter replaced them; they've become a very important land mark, er road sign. Anyway, the paper says it took until Monday with three crews shoveling-one from Monson-one from Shirley-and one from Greenville before they got the road cleared back to Greenville."

The Moose Horns

MONSON, Me., Oct. 17, 1883.

A moose's horns, immense and bleached, guide the wayfarer to the village of Monson. Forty years ago, these honors of some gigantic moose slain in western Piscataquis, were lettered and erected as a guide-board, at a point where the stage road to Monson branches to Blanchard, one noble antler pointing to the one town and its companion to the other. A few days ago, the new narrow gauge railroad began to carry passengers to Monson, and the stage from Abbott has lost its usefulness. Hence, fewer travellers see the mighty spreading horns, five feet from tip to tip and each broad enough for a chairback, than in the times not long past when everybody went to Monson by the stage road.

First newspaper article about Moose Horns

Granny called me over to sit by her at the table and said, "Here's another story for you, Billy," and she pointed to a clipping and started to read:

"'Bunny' MacFarland, a traveling salesman, one day last week attempted to bunt our narrow-gauge train off the track at Monson Junction but could not do it. As luck would have it the train did not have to go to the garage for repairs, but "Bunny" had to take his car there and have a few injuries repaired. This is the second time a car has tried to tip this piece of rolling stock over and Conductor Morrill is getting somewhat nervous about the third attempt."

I suddenly came to back to the present when I took a swallow of coffee and it was stone cold, but I was right-the article was dated 1934.

So I got up and checked on the fire, and on Hattie; her and the cat were very content working on a quilt together. I'm not sure how much help the cat was, but Hattie wasn't complaining, and neither was LC. I scratched the back of the dog's head, poured another shot of coffee, stole a cookie or two from the jar, and sat back down to reminisce some more.

As I was flipping slowly though the book, I realized Granny White's scrapbook was in a lot better order than my memories were.

The wind had stopped but the snow was still falling in big lazy flakes. You know how a long gentle snow with flakes the size of quarters can be so relaxing. As I looked out over the lake everything seemed so still and calm; even the dog seemed to sense a quiet stillness. I took a sip of coffee and looked back down at the scrap book and I saw an article about Conductor Morrill narrowly escaping death. Before I could even start reading the article, my mind took me back to the time when my Grandpa first introduced me to Mr. Morrill.

Harold Morrill wearing his Conductor hat at the Junction

Still, as young as I was at the time, I'm pretty sure it was on that first visit, the one when the train ran out of coal, that I met Mr. Morrill for the first time.

Even though I was young, I was beginning to catch on to my Grandpa's way of telling stories; I always suspected that he'd pull my leg if he got a chance. But after the story of the locomotive running out of coal being true, I was relaxing my guard a bit.

Over and over, I'd been told how good a man Mr. Morrill was, how he was the superintendent of the whole railroad. Sometimes he was the engineer, or the fireman; he sold the tickets to the passengers in the office and then collected them when he was on the train as the conductor. He helped unload the slate at the junction; once in a while he would do the brakeman's job. Once he even worked on the section crew.

Grandpa said he wore more hats than any man he'd ever known, that he was smart and stood as giant among men. Grandpa said he was a pillar of the community. I knew what a giant was, but I wasn't so sure about a pillar.

"What's a pillar, Pa?"

"Why a pillar, is like a tall strong, post that supports things," He replied.

Okay, so here I am, not quite six years old, and I'm on my way to the Monson station to meet a giant among men, as tall as a tree and I had no idea what he looked like, but he could sure wear a lot of hats. I wondered if he had more than one head.

As me and Grandpa turned along Water Street and took the steps leading to the platform, I began to pull back. You know, sort of like a dog that didn't want to walk on a leash.

Grandpa said: "What's a matter with you Billy, Don't you want to meet Mr. Morrill?"

"I'm afraid Pa."

"What in the world are you afraid of? If you want to get a train ride we have to see Mr. Morrill."

"But Pa," and I turned as if to run back home and Gandpa grabbed me.

"Billy, what in tar nation has got into you? Now come on." He opened the door to the station and set me down and I cowered behind his legs.

"Harold, this is my grandson Billy. Now Billy ,shake hands with Mr. Morrill.

Timidly, I stuck my head around his leg and there stood a pleasant looking gentleman wearing a vest and tie and glasses. As he knelt down to shake my hand, I tried to see behind him. But I never did see the giant.

As I took his hand I said, "Where's the giant that has so many heads Pa?"

He laughed, "Sorry, Harold, I was telling Billy how many different hats you wore when doing all the job's you do, and I guess he figured if you could wear so many hats you must have several heads. I told him you were a giant among men."

Harold was kneeling next to me; a big grin appeared on his face, and as he looked up at Grandpa, he laughed as well.

"You can call me Harold, if I can call you Billy," and he stuck out his hand again and said "deal" I grabbed his hand and replied "deal." Then that giant of a man picked me up and gave me a giant of a hug.

Chapter five

a community

It was getting toward supper time, and I'd already had my nap. I'd sort of lost my enthusiasm for working on the railroad, since Karl won't drive fifteen miles through the snow just play trains with me. Even though we thought we were still a couple of boys, we had managed to pick up a little bit of common sense; at least Karl had.

He told me one time when we were working on some kind of project, that I had more common sense than anyone he had ever known.

I turned around puffed my chest out and grinned, until he said: "Because you have obviously never used any!"

Boy, was I deflated!

Still, I have to admit there were plenty of times Hattie would agree with him.

I'd left Granny White's scrapbook open on the table and as I was turning pages and waiting for supper, I realized that she had saved clippings about all kind of things, not just the railroad.

She had saved a clipping from February 6, 1911 headlined:

"MONSON ACADEMY WINS GAME WITH FAST MASSACHUSETTS TEAM".

"The Monson Academy basketball team showed the Tufts 'Independents' five of Medford, Mass., what Maine's fastest preparatory school team could do in a fast and clean game of basketball at Tarr's hall, Saturday evening Feb 4, by defeating them 34 to 18.

The visitors arrived on the 6:50 train, arriving from Belfast...."

Well, I guess there was a slight mention of the train; however,the rest of the article told how proud the whole village was of the Academy team.

"Every seat in the hall was taken early in the evening, and at 9:00 o'clock 325 people were anxious to see these two noted teams go at it.

A round of applause greeted both teams as they came upon the floor and soon the great game was on. The academy boys shot 5 baskets before the

Tarr's Hall later Spencer hall

visitors got started. The half ended 19 to 9 in favor of the home team."

The article gave the final score and listed each player's individual points, the referee's, scorer's and timer's names, then went on:

"The Massachusetts team was somewhat heavier than the local team but very well matched in height. They stayed in town over Sunday leaving Monday morning for Lewiston where they played that evening. A large number enjoyed two hours of

41

dancing after the game. Music by Wilkins and Hughes."

I couldn't tell which team was leaving for Lewiston, but I enjoyed the article.

I put the book down and set the table; I didn't want Hattie to do all of the work when it came mealtime. I'd have helped with the cooking, but we've already discussed how me and the dog felt about that. Hattie's opinion wasn't much better, and nobody had ever asked LC the cat.

When Hattie started setting the food on the table, I slid the book aside and finished setting the drinks on the table. I took her hand across the table, and we thanked the Lord for all we had and asked His blessings on our food. I could tell by Hattie's expression that she had spent a part of her day thinking about times gone by too.

You know, just because you sometimes think about the past doesn't mean you are longing for the good old days. Most times when we think about the past, two things happen: we are reminded of the joy and laughter and fun of family and old friends, and also if you'd lived through any part of the 1930's depression or a war or had survived a serious illness, you became very grateful for all you have now.

Of course, you can find anything if you look hard enough. Hattie and me just prefer to look for good, realizing how blessed we have been. You're welcome to look at things however you choose; still I think most of us older folks choose to remember the good.

When I think back to the kids I'd gone to school with or men I'd met or worked with that are no longer with us, I'm reminded to be a kind, caring, and helpful person to all I meet. We never knew all the things that others went through, but one thing was for sure, none us of could do it on our own.

Hattie turned on the TV to get the 6:00 o'clock news; all I cared about was the weather forecast, and I could get that by looking out the window. The snow was still coming down in big lazy flakes, and the temperature was hoverin' around 28 degrees.

I lifted the lid off the wood box and decided that I'd better fill it one more time before dark. I pulled my boots and coat on, grabbed my hat and gloves, whistled once softly for the dog, and Bella came bouncing toward the door. That dog sure did like to play in the snow, but I could hardly get her outside if it was a fine day. I wondered how she would've faired back in Maine. She probably would have done the same thing she does now, just play in it and have fun.

I shook the snow off the board that covered the top of the wood wagon and pulled the drawer out from the side of the house. I filled the drawer as quickly as I could and left the wagon empty. I knew I'd never pull even an empty wagon up hill to the woodshed in this much snow, so I blazed a trail up to the woodshed and Bella stayed in my tracks as she followed me. I grabbed an arm load of wood and lurched my way to the back porch and unloaded and went back for another load. By the time I was finished with my business, Bella was finished with hers and we went inside.

Hattie met us at the door, and she grabbed Bella up in a towel to dry her off.

As I hung up my coat and hat I said, "I piled some wood up on the porch, because I can't pull the wagon thru the snow, and I'm not going shovel a path until it stops snowing."

She said, "Okay by me; I'm going back to my quilt, the news is over." Her and LC headed back to bedroom, where she had the quilt spread out on the bed.

I turned the TV off and set back down at the table, I was getting to the point where I'd rather read or work on the railroad than watch TV, unless it was a baseball or football game, and here lately, thanks to Karl, I was watching a little college basketball, especially if Purdue was playing.

Boy, I can't believe how quickly I can get off track, and lose what I'm talking about. Sometimes, I miss my mind more than anything else I've ever lost.

Flipping through the scrapbook again, and sipping on my coffee, I ran across an article that brought tears to my eye. The headline said:

"FATALITY BURNED", MARCH 31,1913

"Will Cook, a fireman for the Monson railroad received burns Thursday evening from which died Sunday in the B.M.G. Hospital.

Mr. Cook was building a fire in his kitchen stove about half past four, and used kerosene as was his custom. By some means the oil in the can caught fire and exploded, blowing out the bottom of the can and igniting his clothing, also the room. Mr. Cook kicked a window out and jumped through, running a short distance into a field and back again, tearing his burning clothing from him as best he could.

His cries where heard by neighbors and help soon arrived.....It was decided that he should be taken to the hospital in Bangor, which was done, Dr. Depoe accompanying him.

Mr. Cook was about 38 years old and had been in the employ of the Monson Railroad as fireman on the engine for a number of years."

The article went on to say that damage to the house was not great. It told about his survivors and said that he carried $1000.00 insurance.

I made a mental note not to share this article with Joey until he got a little older, and maybe not at all.

Granny White must have been affected by the story, as I'm sure her and Grandpa knew Mr. Cook and his family. I noticed that right next to the article about Mr. Cook, she had placed an article that was about a happier subject.

"OPERA A SUCCESS"

"The three-act comic opera 'Alvin Gray or The Sailor's Return' presented by local talent under the auspices of the Baptist circle was witnessed by a large and appreciative audience."

The article finished up on pleasant note:

"After the entertainment a social was enjoyed during which ice cream and homemade candies were sold. The receipts of evening was nearly $85.00."

As I was turning the page, a loose article fell out:

ANNIVERSARY OF MONSON BAND

"The 25th anniversary of the Monson Band, the oldest band in Piscataquis County, was observed Thursday evening in the G.A.R. hall. The members of the band were present in uniform and rendered several numbers, including a few of the first pieces the band ever played in public, followed by some late pieces. All former band members and their wives were invited to attend and about fifty were present. Present and former members make a total of more than 80, about half of which are residents of this town."

By the time I'd finished the two, more pleasant, articles my tears had dried up, and it was getting late. I closed the book up, bundled up and took Bella out for a snowy stroll in the dark. With the back porch lights on, reflecting off the snow, it was almost as bright as day time.

When we came back in, Hattie was waiting with the towel again, Bella wasn't exactly liking that, but she got a treat when she was dry.

"Well, if Bella gets a treat when she comes in from the cold, how about we have some dessert?" I asked.

Hattie said, "Great minds think alike; I was just thinking the same thing. How's a piece of apple pie and a scoop of ice cream sound?'

"I'll get the ice cream out of the back freezer," was the only answer she needed.

We sat down across from each other, grinning like a couple kids, like we did over fifty years ago when we'd first gotten married. There is a real comfort that words can't explain, when you are with your wife and friend. Sometimes just being together is enough.

Chapter six

A narrow Escape

Thankfully, the day dawned bright and clear, the new sun sparkling on the snow, and it had warmed up to 32 degrees. The slow-moving storm had passed us by during the night, and Hattie said the next few days were forecast to be in the mid thirty's and mostly clear.

I didn't put a lot of trust in those weather forecasters, but I reckon they were doing the best they could. I remember when I was a kid; Granny White could forecast the weather just by looking at the old flue upstairs in the attic or by rubbing her knees. I never did understand until she told me that if it was going to snow, the old flue would start to sweat and a stain would appear, and it would be snowing by night-fall. She said when her knees started to ache, it meant rain.

She was seldom wrong.

Of course, now that I'm older, I understand how an achy knee full of arthritis can forecast the weather.

The snow was deep enough that I knew the paper wouldn't get delivered, and the wood box was full enough that I didn't have to go outside just yet. Bella had a quick romp outside and was curled up on her bed by the wood stove; LC came up and nudged her over a bit and lay down beside her.

Bella and LC had been raised pretty much together and sometimes LC acted more like a dog than a cat. The two of them got along like an old, married couple, pretty good most of the time, but occasionally they'd snarl at each other a bit.

As I helped dry the breakfast dishes, Hattie told me it was a perfect day to quilt, and if I could find some place else to hang out, she was going to use the table. I grabbed my coffee cup and Granny's scrapbook and moved them out of the way. I carried Hattie's sewing machine into the front room for her. I filled up my coffee cup, picked up the scrap book and Bella and me headed to the railroad room.

I had a few buildings I wanted to paint, and I still had that mill building that Joey had knocked off its foundation to repair. Karl had called on the phone and we discussed a few things about the railroad. I figured I could look through the scrapbook, while I waited for the paint and glue to dry.

When I am working on the Monson layout and looking at some of the buildings Karl and I had built, it is real easy to put myself back into the 1930's when I was a kid. I was remembering meeting Harold Morrill for the first time and picked up the scrap book to see if I could find a picture of him. Then I remembered about the accident he was in. I started looking for the newspaper clipping that I had remembered seeing before.

CONDUCTOR ON MONSON RAILROAD NARROWLY ESCAPES DEATH

(May 26,1910)

"Conductor H. E. Morrill narrowly escaped death on his second trip to Monson Junction Friday afternoon. In making up the train a car load of lumber was attached to the rear and on the down trip Engineer Stevens noticed a hot box on this car. As the train was going down the long grade below the Pullens crossing Stevens signaled to Morrill, who was standing on the steps to the passenger car, to take a look. Conductor Morrill leaned out from the train and was looking back when he was

struck in the head by the hood of the hand car which had been removed from the main line to let the train go by, and as it happened was left so there was just room for the train to pass. Mr. Morrill was stunned by the blow as the train was probably making 20 to 25 miles an hour at this grade and fell to the ground being immediately struck by a spring beneath the car and was rolled over several times and dragged for some distance before the train was stopped. It was found that Mr. Morrill had gone through this and was still alive. At this writing, he is getting along all right, but is very sore and lame and thinks himself lucky that he was not killed or had a leg cut off by the train."

The date of the article was May 26, 1910, seventeen days after Grandpa White went to work for the railroad and Mr. Morrill was nearly killed. I hope my Grandpa wasn't to blame. Guess it's too late to ask him now, but the articles seem to blame the circumstances more than any individual. Well, Mr. Morrill obviously recovered because I met him in 1934 when I was about 6 years old, and he certainly didn't seem to me to be upset with my Grandpa.

There was another interesting article on that page of the scrapbook, and this one came from the *Portland Sunday Telegram.* It wasn't dated, but it must have been from around the same time because Engineer Stan Stevens was still at the throttle.

"...a phone call came to Monson that there was a fire at the Excelsior Mill at Abbot and they wanted the Monson fire engine to come down and help fight the blaze. The pumper was run out of the fire engine house by manpower, loaded onto a flatcar and when the 8P.M. train came in everything was ready to couple on and go back to Monson Junction with the apparatus. Stan Stevens was at the throttle of the engine and a record run was made over the six miles of narrow gauge rails. Horses were waiting at the junction to haul the engine to the scene of the fire and as a matter of fact the old wooden covered bridge over the Piscataquis River was saved. Many other times the little railroad proved its worth in emergencies.

That last sentence *"Many other times the little railroad proved its worth in emergencies."* really says a lot. It says a lot about the spirit of the railroad and the spirit of Monson Village as well. To me it tells the story of small-town family life, where neighbors help neighbors. Funny, my youth was spent between Bangor and Monson, and other than a few school friends from Bangor, most all of my memories are about Monson.

I remember Mr. Morrill setting me up in the cab of #3 the day I first met him and getting to blow the whistle. I remember Grandpa White introducing me to Elwin French, the engineer and Albin Johnson ,the fireman. I remember meeting Cecil Johnson. He was on the track crew with Grandpa; he was the youngest man on the crew. I think everybody in town was sad when he got sick and died in 1939; he was only 22 years old. I remember especially because he died in August two days before my 11th birthday.

"Billy! Are you going stay out there playing trains all day, I declare, you'd rather work on that railroad than eat" Hattie called from the railroad door "Come in here and let's have some dinner"
Well, Bella must have smelled something she wanted, because she flew up those stairs"
I knew better than to pass up instructions like these; otherwise I'd be eating my own cooking again, and we've discussed that issue already.

I don't know how we got in the habit of calling it breakfast, dinner and supper; maybe because that was what Granny White always called it. Of course, it didn't really matter what you called them; anybody who sees me could tell by looking that I hadn't missed too many meals.

I'd done a pretty good job of wasting the early part of the day, and these winter days were short, but somehow the wood box kept getting emptied out, even if it wasn't snowing. I figured I'd better get it filled up before Hattie gave me another set of instructions that I couldn't refuse.

So after I'd carried the wood from the back porch in, me and Bella headed out to the wood shed. I still couldn't pull the wagon through the snow, so it was back and forth from the wood shed to the wood box. Eventually, Bella got tired of walking back and forth with me, so she climbed up on the porch to watch.

That was just as well, she wasn't helping anyway. I couldn't get her to fetch a stick; I don't know why I thought she'd carry even a small piece of fire wood. Finally, I had tromped the snow down enough that I could pull the wagon over it. 'Course by that time I'd filled it up one-arm load at a time, and there was no point in moving it. I put the wooden cover on it and weighted it down so none of the four strong winds would blow it off.

I figured I'd earned my afternoon nap; Bella agreed with me, so that is what we did. As I was drifting off I got to thinking about the big snow roller that used to pack the snow on the roads back in Monson. Maybe I'd build me a miniature snow roller and teach Bella to pull it and I wouldn't have to shovel a path for the wood wagon.

I decided the best course of action would be to sleep on it a bit.

Chapter seven

never give up

Have you ever noticed that the older you get the more mysterious some things become? I thought we were supposed to get wiser with age. Here's another question for you, do you think more about the hereafter now that you are older?

Well, I sure do. I go into the living room and I wonder what I'm here after, I go into the kitchen and I wonder what I'm here after, same thing in the railroad room or the shop. At least I can remember what I'm after when I go into the bathroom......my hearing aids.

But, the mystery I'm trying to solve now is how eight or ten inches of snow can stop a modern-day mail carrier like it does. Here is an article from 1911.

"There have been notices in the news columns of several surrounding towns about the R.F.D. mail

carrier missing only one day in the recent heavy snows and high winds. The subscribers on the route which starts in Abbot Village and goes through the southwest part of Monson are very proud of their mail carrier, Robert Morse, of Abbot, as he has not lost a trip thus far this winter. There is but one other person who passes over several miles of the road this winter, so Mr. Morse does not find a much traveled road. However, he is one of those who never say 'Give Up.'"

Well, I guess I shouldn't be too hard on the mail carriers of today; after all, I didn't want to pull the wood wagon a couple of hundred feet uphill in the snow. 'Course, I am racking up the years, and Hattie's even is older than me. Don't tell her I said so, but the truth is she's got me by 10 days. It used to be a lot of fun to kid her about being married to an older woman, but now she's in better shape than me. Come to think about it, she's always had a better shape than me.

Of course, neither one of us has given up yet on our responsibilities; we still get things done....eventually. I can remember when Grandpa White was trying to teach me about life, and he told me that there was one thing that I didn't have to worry about ever running out of. He said that in his time he had run out of gas, out of food, out of money, out of firewood, out of fishin' worms, out of clean clothes, out kerosene and once he had been on a train that ran out of coal, and that someday he'd probably run out of time; but never yet had he run out of work to be done.

At least, that was one lesson that I was taking to heart: what I didn't get done today would still be there tomorrow. As far as I can tell there's only a couple of differences between being retired and still being employed: I don't have to start work until I'm good and ready, and I can quit whenever I want to. Of course, the money isn't the same either.

Hattie reminded me that some of that work I'd been saving was still waiting for me, and maybe it would be a good idea to get started on it. Well, you can forget that part about me not having to start working until I was good and ready.

I remembered telling the kids when all five of them were still home how-when I was at home-I was the undisputed boss, and Nan said,"yeah, but Mom..." I held my hand and, "Nan, I said when I'm home I am the boss."

She tried again, "yeah, but Mom said...."

"Nancy Ann, when I am home I am the boss, you got it?"

"Okay," all of the kids replied timidly.

Then I said, "And when we are both home, Mom's the boss".

The forecast was for high winds and more snow; I got right to work filling the wood box and taking out the trash. As usual Bella wasn't much help, but we got the job done. Naturally, I left a little work for later just in case.

Even though it wasn't snowing yet, it was hovering at 30 degrees, and it didn't take long for these old hands and toes to get cold. Hattie was in the back of the house and I hollered at her (maybe that's were Nancy gets some of that loudness from). "I'll be in the railroad room."

Don't know why I bothered to tell her, she knew where to find me if I wasn't in her sight, and she knew it wasn't likely I'd miss a meal.

As I was walking past the front window, I glanced at the lake; there wasn't a ripple on it. I stepped out on the front porch for a minute and the air had an eerie, still feeling to it. My old bones were telling me we were headed for some kind of storm. It felt like the sky had just taken in a real deep breath, and when it exhaled, well, who could knew what would happen.

I didn't linger and made sure the door was firmly shut behind me.

For some reason, I just couldn't seem to leave Granny White's scrapbook alone; guess I was trying to stay ahead of Joey. Any way I found another article about those old-time railroaders and how they never gave up:

"February 13, 1911 it takes more than breaking of a piston-rod and the blowing out of a cylinder head on the engines of the Monson railroad to stop train service, which happened to both engines last Thursday afternoon. In the early part of the day one of the engines was in the Monson-Maine quarry the piston rod broke and pushed through the cylinder-head. In the meantime the 8:55 train had gone to the Junction and the superintendent was wired that the engine had met with the same kind of an accident. Superintendent Morrill, who is also a master mechanic of the road, went to work on the engine which was at the quarry disabled and after several hours had it fixed so that it could be used. The other engine was fixed up the same way and then both were coupled together and the two could haul the passenger coach. The connections were made all right with the afternoon train of the B.&A. and with the last up train. It may seem quite a story but it is a fact that sixty were taken aboard the passenger car on the night train up from the junction and the next morning sixty-eight."

As soon as I'd finished this story, I realized that here was Mr. Morrill with another hat, master mechanic of the railroad. Memories of my child -hood came flooding back, and I got to laughing at myself when I thought about being afraid of the "many headed giant."

Chapter eight

fire and wind

I remember one fall day in early October, I don't remember the year, but Marie hadn't been born yet. Dad took me and Vernon and Mom to the Bangor & Aroostook station, we were gonna take the train west to Monson Junction and meet Granny and all of us ride the narrow gauge up to Monson. I guess my daddy figured that was easier than him driving up and back twice. Plus we went up in the middle of the week and Mom would only have to stay until Saturday, and then I could be the boss of Vernie.

This was the first train ride for Vernie, and the first time I'd been on the standard gauge myself. Anyway, when we were walking up to the platform, my hat blew off. As I was chasing my hat, just before it blew on to the tracks, a man caught it for me. He handed it back to me, I said "Thanks Mr."

and then I asked , "does the wind blow this way all the time down here?"

"No" he pointed over his left shoulder and said, "part of the time it blows from that way over there."

You know, the human mind is an incredible thing. One little jog, and it can take you miles away from where you are, or maybe miles away from where you thought you were headed.

Well, before I got blown so far of course, I was going to tell you about another swirling wind.

I had often watched my Grandpa White build the fire in the stove. I knew how he would whittle a few shavings off a piece of kindling, and stack things just right, then strike the match and set it on the shavings. I guess I was eight or nine, and I wanted to help Granny out, so I was going to build the fire for her; I knew Grandpa would be proud of me.

But what if I couldn't get it to start right, maybe I'd practice outside by Granny's truck farm. So I snuck into the house and took a couple matches and the whittling knife from beside the wood stove. I grabbed a couple of pieces of kindling and headed around the chicken coop.

Now, I'm sure you remember me telling you about Granny White's pretty hazel eyes, and how they saw what I was fixing to do before I even did it. As I was sneaking around the chicken coop, Granny saw me through the kitchen window, and she quietly followed me. I was very intent on the task set before me, and I didn't know she was watching.

I carefully whittled a little pile of shavings, stacked the kindling just like I'd seen Grandpa do and was ready to strike the match. Well, the wind was swirling around a bit, and my first match blew out. I didn't know it at the time, but Granny's eyes were getting bigger when she realized what I was planning to do.

I struck the second match and it blew out also. I turned around to go get some more matches, and when I saw Granny standing there, my eyes got big too. Before I could explain, she reached down and picked up Grandpa's knife with one hand and grabbed me by the ear with the other. And we proceeded quickly into the house; maybe I should say she "marched" me into the house.

She said nary a word until she had set me down at the table, put Grandpa's knife back and then she said, "Young man, you stay right there and I'm going read to you from the book." Usually when Grandpa or my dad was going to "read to me from the book", it meant a couple of swats on my bottom end. She moved toward the bureau, and then I thought she was going to pick up the Bible and tell me what the Jesus had to say about what I had done. Instead she picked up her scrapbook, and she was flipping through it she asked me just what I had been planning to do.

I explained my whole plan, how I was going to save Grandpa some work, and how I knew he'd be proud of me and I was just going practice outside first. She wondered if I knew how dangerous fire was, and I told her of course I knew I could get burned, that was why I was being so careful to practice first.

She shook her head, "That's not what I'm talking about. You listen to this story and it'll teach you how dangerous fire is."

MONSON R.R. SUFFERS $25,000 LOSS

"The Monson Railroad Co. suffered a loss of about $25,000 early Monday morning, Nov. 3 (1919) when their round house containing three engines No.1, No.3 and No.4 was burned to the ground.

The fire was discovered between 12 and 1 o'clock and when the first men arrived on the scene it had such headway that nothing could be saved and all three engines, together with the workshop, were soon laid flat by the flames.

No.1 engine has been in the service of the railroad since it was built 36 years ago, and a few years ago No.3 was purchased, No. 2 being dismantled at this time, and about a year ago No. 4 was bought. Although the distance to Monson Junction is but six miles the towns people feel that it is a hard blow, as the road is the means of freight coming and going out. Both the Monson Maine Slate Co. and the Portland-Maine Slate Co. will feel the loss if the road should be tied up for any length of time, as slate shipments are being made nearly every day and just at this time sand and coal are coming in.

How the fire started is a mystery as two of the engines had no fire in them and the third one had a light fire built about 6 0'clock Sunday night.

Up to Monday night no definite plans were made for the future. Work was commenced Monday to right N0.4 and it is believed this engine can be repaired so to run in a short time. For the present passengers, mail and express will be conveyed to and from Monson Junction by automobile."

I set there quietly, letting it all sink in. Fire had burned up the whole round house and three engines. I must've had a shocked expression on my face, because Granny just sat there and watched me, waiting for my reaction. Finally, struggling to hold back my tears, I told her how sorry I was, and that I'd let Grandpa build the fire after all.

"Would you like a cookie and some milk?" Granny asked me, "I've got another story to read you about fires."

"Yes, please." I answered quietly.

"You stay put, and I'll be right back."

I wasn't about to move; so far I didn't seem to be in too bad a trouble, but I wasn't taking any chances.

She came back in the room, set a plate of cookies and a glass of milk on the table, and picked up her scrapbook again. Then she began to read, "FROM THE OBSERVER NOVEMBER 6, 1924" she paused and said, "My goodness, I never noticed this before This article is almost exactly five years after the round-house fire, it missed by only three days."

She looked at me and asked what I thought about that. I didn't know what to think, so I just stuck another cookie in my mouth and shook my head.

She continued reading, *"Considerable excitement was occasioned here Friday, when it was discovered that the train on its return from the Junction at noon had set a fire which was burning the edge of the William Partinen woods. Had it not been for the help which arrived promptly the fire would have been serious, for the woods are full of tops from old cuttings as well as good lumber. Again on Saturday, while burning the right of way the fire got beyond the control of the section men and burned over a part of the Day and Knight Places and was again in the edge of the woods before being controlled. This time Fire Warden Harry Davis was notified. It is very dry now and forest fires will be prevented only with extreme precaution."*

As the reality of what I had nearly done set in, with a horrified gasp I said, "Granny, I might have burned the chicken coup and house down. I guess the wind blowing out my matches saved me."

She smiled and said, "You should be very thankful you didn't get burnt and neither did anything else. You know Billy, sometimes God works in mysterious ways."

I never did tell Grandpa White what I had done; I don't think Granny did either. When it dawned on me that I didn't get a swat, I had to agree with Granny. God does work in mysterious ways!

Chapter nine

strange cargo

I was finally getting used to the idea of having a little brother; I really didn't have much choice, besides I had a ready playmate. I was five years older than Vernon

And then when he was two years old, Mom came home with our little sister. Me and Vernie weren't real sure about having a sister, but nobody asked us. Her name was Marie, she was okay when she got a little older, but it was tough getting used to having her around.

The best time to visit with Grandpa and Granny White was during the early summer. It wasn't too hot, and the days were long; sometimes Mom would stay with us for a week or so. Mom and Granny would gather the three of us kids up and we'd walk down to Water Street and over to Main street. Once in a while we'd get a piece of penny candy from the A. & P., but most of the time we'd go over to the shore of Hebron Pond, and me and Vernie could fish.

Of course being the big brother I had to help Vernie bait his hook, that wasn't too bad until Marie had to fish too.

You ever seen a three-year-old girl in pig tails try to fish?

Mom said I had to let Marie use my pole, so I spent my fishing time baiting everybody's hooks and complaining about why Marie had to fish in the first place.

Then Marie let out a little scream and started running away from the water, dragging the fishing pole behind her. Me and Vernie turned around and watched in amazement as she dragged the biggest splake we'd ever seen right out of the water and up the bank behind her. I practically had to tackle her to get her to stop running and screaming.

Finally, I got my pole back and me and Vernie each caught a couple of brown trout, and he caught another splake and we headed home. I told Vernie the reason he caught more fish than me was because I was an expert at baiting hooks, and I had given him extra special worms. I think maybe some of that leg-pulling Grandpa did when he was telling stories was rubbing off on me.

Even though Grandpa still had to work long hours since he'd been working on the railroad, the walk home from the engine house wasn't so far and he never seemed to be as tired after work, as he used to be. Grandpa cleaned the fish when he got home, and we all had fried potatoes and fish for supper. Granny made a mess of greens from her truck farm, and we all ate until the fish was gone.

I wanted a glass of milk with dinner, but Grandpa said, "Now Billy you know that fish don't swim in milk, they swim in water, and if you drank milk while you're eating fish, why your stomach would be flipping and flopping around something fierce, and you'd have to go straight to bed until it stopped"

I looked at Mom and Granny, but they just shrugged their shoulder and I settled for water; I wasn't taking any chances about having to go to bed right after dinner.

I still remember that summer evening, after the fish fry.

It was a Saturday evening and Mom and Granny were fixing strawberry shortcake. Vernie and Grandpa and me were sitting on the front porch steps. I guess Marie was already asleep. I knew she was tired after her day of fishing, Mom had carried her all the way home from town. At least it was downhill.

Anyway Grandpa wanted to know if me and Vernie wanted to hear a story.

Vernie said, "yeah, Pa."

I wondered, "Is it about the railroad, Pa?"

Grandpa started out, "Well, it's not really a story, but it's about the railroad."

Together me and Vernie sang out, "But, Pa!"

"Now you two young'uns hold on just a second. It's not a story because it's what really happened. As a matter of fact, it happened this very day not more than four or five hours ago." and he paused to light his pipe.

"Really, Grandpa, today?" Vernie chimed in before I could ask; now that boy should have a little more respect for his elders. But before I could straighten Vernie out, Grandpa continued.

"Now Vernon (I thought Grandpa was going to lecture him, but instead he said), you won't know this spot on the railroad, 'cause you've never been there on the motor car. But you'll get your chance when you get a little older. Billy knows where it's at, don't you, Billy?"

I'm not sure I knew what he was talking about, but I sure wasn't going let Vernie know that, so I replied heartily, "I sure do Grandpa!"

"Now Billy, I haven't even told you where the fire was yet, so how can you know?"

"S" curve with cattle underpass

At the word fire, a fear began to crawl up my back, my belly started hurting, and I was thinking maybe I should have went to bed right after supper. I was holding my breath; I figured I was gonna get that swat I didn't get from before, and then I remembered he said that it had happened this very day.

With a sigh of relief I spit out, "Sorry Pa, guess I got a little excited and got ahead of things."

"That's alright. Now Jim Crockett-you know Jim, he's the section chief-anyway, Jim, T.P. and me were down by the big S curve replacing a couple ties just this side of the bridge."

I saw a chance to impress my little brother, so I jumped in, "You mean that bridge that the cows can go under so the train don't hit 'em, Grandpa?"

"That's the one, Billy. Now try not to interrupt me or I'll forget what I'm talking about, and we might miss out on those strawberrys and shortcake. Well, we'd just about finish up and was getting ready to move to the other side of the bridge, when we heard number four coming down grade."

I was in luck this time Vernie wanted to know how Grandpa knew it was number four, so I didn't get in trouble for interrupting.

"Vernie, each locomotive has its own special whistle, so you can tell by the sound which locomotive it is. And I'll tell you something else; you can tell which Engineer is running the loco, by his special touch on the whistle. But that's not what this story is about.

(Gee, Vernie didn't even get in trouble for interrupting.)

So the three of us pulled the trailer and motor car off the track and stepped back away from the track. When we had heard the whistle, I bet T.P. that Elwin French was behind the throttle today, and-sure enough-as the train went by, Elwin waved.

Then we turned and looked and behind the loco were two flat cars loaded with the strangest looking pieces of slate we had ever seen. Now mind you, we were used to seeing all kinds of slate, crated slate, uncrated slate, stacked loose, we'd seen piles of pulpwood, and finished lumber and all kinds of things, but nothing like this.

I mean to tell you they were long, so long that they took up almost the whole car, and so wide that you couldn't see over them from the ground. We guessed that they were at least an inch thick. They must have been really heavy, because two flat cars were all number four could handle.

The train went by, and as the last car went over the bridge and cleared the other side, Jim saw a burst of flame and a puff of smoke and yelled out 'Fire on the Bridge!' A spark from the loco must have started the fire.

We pulled the motor car and trailer back onto the track as quickly as we could; I gave it a crank and off we raced to the fire. When we got there, T.P. and me jumped off with our shovels, one on each side of the track; Jim pulled the motor car and trailer out of harm's way, and raced to the edge of the woods.

It was a pretty busy there for a while, but we got the fire out before it could spread to the woods; however the bridge was partly destroyed.

Motor car that Elwin French built

Jim climbed down under the bridge to inspect the damage. When he came back up he said, 'We better get down to the Junction and give Morrill a call; I don't think we can run a train over it until we replace a couple of the stringers."

Grandpa paused to relight his pipe. Vernie and me were on the edge of our seats, one on each side of Grandpa.

"Then what happened, Pa?" Vernie asked before I could; I definitely need to tell that boy about respect, maybe later.

"We sat the trailer off the rails and out of the way," Grandpa continued. "Then we cranked up the motor car and headed for the Junction as fast as the little car could go. We stopped at the station and Jim got off and went to see Mr. Crozier, the BAR station agent, to get him to call Superintendent Morrill.

Number four was backing the two flatcars onto the transfer track, as T.P. and me pulled to a stop to watch. I got off and ran across the weeds to where I could pass along the news about the fire damaging the bridge. Cecil Johnson was working as the brakeman that day, and he waved to me as he was finishing up uncoupling. We met beside the track and walked up to the engine together. We climbed up into the cab, and Elwin pulled the loco down off the transfer track.

I explained what was happening, as he was pulling the loco over to the water tank siding. By that time Jim had made his call and was walking down the track to meet us. He climbed on the motor car and him and T.P. pulled on to the siding behind us.

'Elwin, guess Clarence told you about the bridge? Well Howard said for you to leave the lokie here and come home with us. I'm sure the bridge will hold the car. We'll come down at first light and make the repairs, and we should be good by tomorrow afternoon.

Number Four and her crew

So six of us Cecil, T.P., Elwin, Frank Hughes, the fireman, Jim and me, all climbed on the motor and headed back to pick up the trailer. Jim asked Cecil, what in the world they had been hauling, and he told him they were switchboards, 122 inches long, 52 inches wide and 1 inch thick"

Grandpa finished the story by asking us if we knew how long 122 inches was in feet.

But before Vernie or me could show our ignorance, Mom and Granny showed up with the strawberry shortcake.

Chapter ten

Truth or consequences

In the early thirties, we lived in the country outside of Bangor, it was kind of poor neighborhood.   There weren't a lot of houses on the gravel road, but kinda catty-cornered from our house was a big two story house. At least it seemed big at the time.   We had a one story framed house, with a long dirt driveway, that ran beside a big old Maple tree in the front yard.

In that big old two story lived my friends Ralphie and David. Ralphie was older than me and David, and sometimes he'd play tricks on us or talk us into doing something we shouldn't do.

Well, one time my mom caught us doing something we shouldn't have been doing, I knew better, but I didn't want to let David down, so I went along anyway, hoping I wouldn't get caught, but I did.

At any rate, Mom said that when my daddy got home from work, I was going really be in trouble.

When my daddy got home, he poured himself a cup of coffee and sat down at the table. He called me over, and as I stood by him, he asked me.

"What did you do today Billy?"

"I played with Ralphie and David"

"Well, Billy, what exactly were you playing?"

I looked down and my feet, and replied "Oh just things."

"Now Billy look at me and tell me what you were doing." but before I could reply, he spun me around and pulled a pipe out of my back pocket and said "can you tell me where this came from?" and he laid the pipe on the table.

"I um I'm not sure."

"I see, so you are not sure, but it was in your pocket."

"I think it was Ralphie's."

"Well, you think its Ralph's did Ralph put it in our pocket?"

"Maybe, David did."

He stood up, towering over me, he unbuckled his belt and pulled it out of his pants, and he never said a word. Then he coiled the belt up and set in on the table next to the pipe.

"Did you steal the pipe? Were you smoking the pipe?"

I was silent.

Calmly daddy said, "I want an answer Billy"

I didn't know how to answer, so I stayed mute.

He knelt down in front of me, took me by my shoulders and made me look him in the eye.

"Billy, stealing is one of the worst things you can do, and I will not a tolerate it, do you understand that?"

I could feel the tears welling up, but I nodded my head and stuttered "Yesss."

"But even worse than stealing, Billy, is lying. Every one of us does things wrong or makes mistakes, but when you lie about it you just make things worse. Now turn around."

As I was turning around, I saw him reach for his belt and I knew what was coming. When it was over he told me to take the pipe back to Ralph and get my backside straight back home, because he had some chores for me.

Now, I think Vernie was just starting to walk at the time, so I guess I was six or a little older. And being a typical rambunctious boy, it wasn't long until I was in trouble again. I know exactly what I was in trouble for; it's something I'll never forget.

This time I was on my own, I was playing in our yard, and Mom came out and told me to come take the trash out to the burn barrel. I told her I was busy and that I didn't want to.

She told me again and I said "Damn it to hell, I told you I don't want to do it."

Not another word was spoken, she grabbed me by the ear and I promptly did as I was told.

I thought that would be the end of it, especially since she gave me a swat and almost twisted my ear off, but I was wrong.

When dad got home, he poured himself a cup of coffee and sat down at the table. He called me over, and as I stood by him, he asked me.

"What did you do today Billy?"

"Just stayed home and played in the yard."

"I see," then he stood up and as he was taking his belt off he asked me, "did you cuss at you mom today when she told you to take out the trash?"

My eyes were getting big, as he rolled the belt up and put it on the table.

"Na", I started to reply, and then I remembered his talk about telling the truth, and in mid-word I said "yes daddy I did, I'm sorry"

"Well, did you tell your mother you were sorry?"

"No" I stammered, my gaze shifting back and forth from the belt to his face.

"Billy, go tell your mother you are sorry and that you'll never cuss at her again, and then come right back here."

I found mom on the back porch folding clothes "Mommy, I'm sorry I cussed at you today and I promise I'll never ever do it again."

She smiled and said "Apology accepted, Billy, let me see your ear. It's still a little red, but I think it'll be okay. I'm sorry if it hurts"

"That's ok mom I guess I had it coming, but I gotta go Daddy want's me."

I raced back to the kitchen table, I knew what was coming, and I wanted to get it over with.

Dad pulled out a chair for me and told me to have a seat. He said, he was going to have cookie with his coffee, would I like a cookie too.

Now, I didn't know what to expect, but in spite of my fear of what was coming, I said, "Yes please." I just couldn't bring myself to pass up a cookie, no matter what. (Come to think of it, I still can't.)

I sat there silently eating my cookie, watching dad, and waiting. I finished my cookie and he finished his.

"Well, Billy looks like you still got an hour or so to play before supper, why don't you go on and play."

Now try to picture this if you can. In those days we didn't have aluminum screen doors like we have today, we had wooden doors that were like a hollow wooden rectangle with screen wire stretched across it. In the center was one thin horizontal board that you could push on to open it from inside the house.

Hooked to that center board was a big long spring, it was about ½" in diameter and about a foot long. When the door was pushed wide open, it stretched out to about two and one-half feet. And when you let go of the door it let the screen door close with "BANG!"

So here is this six year old boy, who just escaped a spanking, tearing through the house, pushing the front door wide open and letting it go as he sprints down that long driveway. Just as the door slams shut with a "BANG!" he comes to a skidding stop and turns back to look at the house.

As he is turning, the light bulb is coming on and he's thinking "Wow, when I lie, I get a spanking, when I tell the truth I don't."

Then his gaze comes to rest on his Mom and Dad standing in the front window looking at him. Dad's got his arm around Mom's shoulder, they both smile and wave.

I smiled back and waved, looked both ways before I crossed the road, and disappeared up Ralphie and David's drive way. Lesson learned, honestly is the best policy.

I read in a book somewhere that "the truth shall set you free."

baked beans

Another day, up in Monson, Mom had left Marie with Granny, and Mom, Vernie and me walked up to Hebron Pond. We were going to do some real fishing. But as we turned the corner on to Water Street, the old saw mill behind the G.A.R. Building was humming right along. It sure was noisy, what with the water rushing through the flume, and saw blade singing, and the workers yelling to be heard above all the other noise. The air above the mill was so thick with saw dust it was like it was covered with its own dark cloud.

I was pretty interested in the saw mill, but Mom was nervous about us boys getting too close. She said we could just go home if we didn't want to fish. I think mom was getting home sick, because she was a little bit sad and grouchy.

Most of time if she came up to Granny's with us, her and Marie would only stay one week. I don't remember why, but there must have been a good reason, but this time she had decided to stay for two weeks.

I think it was 1937 or 1938, and I know my daddy was really working hard to take care of all of us. There was this thing called the great depression going on, and in Europe, Germany and Italy had already taken aggressive actions against other nations. I remember the grownups talking about Japan invading China, and maybe we were headed to another war.

All that seemed pretty far away from me and my family, I didn't even know where Japan was, but I knew where Europe was, cause I'd studied about the the Great War in school. Still it seem to worry my Mom a lot, she said Dad was just the right age, but I didn't know what she meant.

Today was only Wednesday, so she had two more days before Dad would get here Saturday some time. I didn't necessarily want Mom to go back home, but I didn't like to see her worried.

I tried not to let it show too much, but I really did like Vernie, and I think he liked me. Sometimes, me and him would just make up stories and games to play by ourselves. Mostly, we had fun, but like Mom, once and while, one of the other of us would get a little grouchy.

The fishing wasn't very good that morning, and us boys were getting hungry, so well before noon we headed back to Granny's house. As we were coming down Water Street around the bend before Chapin Ave, we heard the whistle of the train coming in.

"Mommy, can we go down to the station and watch the train come in?" Both Vernie and me wondered at the same time, "Pretty please."

"Billy, you hold Vernie's hand and don't get too close."

We were off like a shot; we made it to the station platform, huffing and puffing for breath and as excited as only little boys can be. The little locomotive was running backward pushing the combine in front of it and behind it; it was pulling a flatcar and boxcar.

"My Goodness, would you look at that!" a woman behind us exclaimed.

There were people sitting on top of the boxcar, there were people standing and sitting on the flat car; you could tell by looking through the windows that the combine was full; people were standing on its little platform. There was even one man standing in the door way of the baggage compartment. Everybody seemed to be happy, they were all laughing and waving, so we waved back.

Mr. Morrill stepped out of the office on to the platform and stood beside me and Vernie.

"How you doing today, Billy?" he asked.

"Just fine, Mr. I mean Harold. This is my little brother Vernon, he's only five. Shake hands with Mr. Morrill, Vernie."

Mom had caught up to us by this time and she said, "Hello, Harold, what's the special occasion; I've never seen so many people on the train before?"

"It is the Piscataquis County Teachers Convention. These are the teachers from Shirley and Greenville, and the noon train will bring in the speakers. We had nearly 80 passengers on this train. Opal, I haven't seen much of you this visit, Are you bringing the boys and Marie to the five o'clock baked beans supper at Masonic banquet rooms?" Harold inquired, "Everyone is invited."

Before Mom could answer the train came to a stop and the platform and street in front of the station were full of people. Everybody was laughing and hugging and shaking hands; it was like everybody knew everybody else. Mr. Morrill seem to know all of the locals as well as he knew our family.

"Perhaps we'll see you at the supper, Harold," Mom said as we were leaving.

She leaned over to me "Billy, did I hear you call Mr. Morrill Harold?" she practically hissed at me.

"Yeah, Mom," I answered.

"Billy, you know better than that. His name is Mr. Morrill, he is a very important man."

"But Mom, we made a deal."

"Who made a deal, Billy?"

"Me and Harold made a deal. Honest, Mom ,ask Grandpa. We even shook hands on it."

"Who shook hands, Billy?"

"Me and Harold, ask Grandpa.

"Oh, you can be sure I will. I've never been so embarrassed" she said between clinched teeth.

Well, we didn't make the Baked Bean supper, and Grandpa was pretty late getting home from work, but Mom was waiting for him.

"Dad," she began in a very serious tone, "What exactly is this 'deal' that Billy says he shook hands with Mr. Morrill about?"

Vernie was all ears and eyes; I think he was expecting somebody to get a swat and it wasn't gonna be him.

"Billy, tell your mother about your deal with Harold." Grandpa instructed me.

"I did, Grandpa, two times, I told her me and Harold had made a deal and shook on it and everything."

"Well, Opal, the boy told you! Why are you asking me?"

"Dad, he—Billy I mean—" (I could tell mom was getting a little flustered) was calling The Railroad Superintendent by his first name. I'll not cotton to my son being disrespectful."

"Sweetheart, listen, Billy is not being disrespectful. Have you ever heard Billy call any other adult by their first name? No, of course you haven't. But Harold and Billy have a deal; they gave each other their word that they would call each other by their first names. As a matter of fact, it was Harold's idea, wasn't it Billy?"

"Yes sir, it sure was, I remember. He knelt down and smiled at me and then stuck his hand out and said 'can I call you Billy?' and I said yes and then he said 'okay, but you've got to call me Harold, deal?' and I said 'deal' and we shook hands and then he picked me up and gave me a giant hug."

"Is that the truth, Dad? When was this deal anyway? How come I've never heard of it before now?" Mom was even more flustered.

Granny was standing in the kitchen doorway listening to the conversation as she was drying her hands after finishing the dishes. She answered, "You didn't hear about it before now, because you weren't here. You were down in Bangor delivering Vernon. Half the town heard the story about Billy and Harold's deal."

Vernie forgot about somebody getting a swat and wanted to hear the story; for that matter Mom did too.

"Billy, tell the story." Granny said.

So I did, I told how I thought Harold was really a giant who had six heads, and that he was as tall as a tree that supported the whole sky. Mom looked pretty confused, Grandpa was practically rolling on the floor laughing, Granny went into the kitchen snickering, and Vernie was saying, "Huh—what—a giant?" as he was looking from one adult to another.

Mom wisely decided to let the subject drop. Even though she was an adult with kids of her own, she still couldn't get ahead of her parents. Seems kids seldom do.

Our daddy arrived that Saturday afternoon, and early the next morning, everybody but me and Vernie headed back to Bangor.

Daddy told me take good care of my little brother. Then he knelt down, smiled at me and said "deal?" and stuck out his hand. I said "deal" and shook his hand. Then he gave me a hug.

As they were driving off, I wondered how he could know about my deal with Harold.

Chapter twelve

mysteries and mishaps

When I woke up that next Saturday morning, my Daddy was sitting at the table with Grandpa White. They were both drinking coffee, Daddy, out of his favorite mug, and Grandpa out of a saucer like he always did. Grandpa always liked his coffee with lots of canned milk in it. He swirled it around in his saucer to cool it down, then he'd sip out of the saucer.

I knew I was dreaming because my Daddy and Mom were supposed to be in Bangor for another week; besides, his favorite mug was at home. And I didn't think I could sleep a whole week.

Grandpa said, "Well, good morning, Big Guy." Grandpa called me Big Guy lots of times.

And my Daddy turned around and pulled me close for a hug. "Well, I thought you were going to sleep all day."

I hugged him back and stammered "Are you really here Daddy? Is this a dream?"

"Yes, son, I'm really here and so is your Mother and Marie. We've got a surprise for you."

"You're not bringing home another little sister, are you?" I wondered with alarm.

"No, not this time." He chuckled. "It's not that kind of a surprise. When your Mom and Vernie are up, I'll tell you all about it."

Just then Granny came out of the kitchen and set a cup of hot chocolate on the table and told me to sit down with the rest of the men. That made me feel pretty grown up.

I listened to Daddy and Grandpa talk about the weather, and somebody named FDR, and a thing call the new deal. Finally, I caught on that they were talking about President Roosevelt.

But that still didn't help me solve the mystery of why my Mom and Dad were here. I knew better than to interrupt or ask questions: I sure wished Mom and Vernie would get up; I think I was getting a little nervous, whatever that was. Mom sometimes got a little nervous too, so maybe that's where I got it from.

Finally, Mom came into the dinning room carrying Marie, and Vernie rubbing his eyes was right behind her. She gave Dad a little kiss and said good morning to the rest of us.

"Can I have my surprise now, Daddy?" I felt like I'd been holding my breath and I finally exhaled. "Please."

"Just you hold on a minute Billy. Let your Mom get a cup of coffee and everybody sit down; then we'll talk," he replied.

Vernie jumped in and asked "Are we going back to Bangor now?"

Mom looked at Dad; he smiled and looked from me to Vernie and then to Grandpa and Granny.

"No Vernie." He began, "No, we aren't going back to Bangor for quite awhile. You and Billy and Marie and Mom are going to be staying with Granny and Grandpa for a while."

I was shocked, and I think Vernie was too, but none of the adults seemed upset, so we just listened.

Daddy continued, "I have a new job, a job that I've always wanted, but I have to go away and go to school for awhile to be trained to do it."

"What kind of job, Daddy?" I jumped in before Vernie could ask.

"I going to learn how to fly an airplane."

Vernie and me chorused together "An Airplane! Really?"

"Really," Mom answered, "and we are all going stay with Granny and Grandpa until Daddy comes back after he finishes his school. Won't that be fun?"

I looked at Vernie and he looked at me; neither one of us was real sure exactly what was happening, but Mom and Daddy and Granny and

Grandpa were all smiling, so we shook our heads yes.

It was beautiful summer morning, a gentle breeze, an early August day, without a cloud in the sky. Granny fixed a big breakfast with biscuits and gravy and eggs and bacon.

After breakfast, all of us menfolk moved outside to start unloading Dad's Model T. I didn't know that old car could hold all that stuff, plus Dad had rigged some kind of trailer on the back. Seemed like everything we owned was on that car.

At almost 10 years old I was big enough to help some, but Vernie was mostly in the way. I admit he sure tried too, but finally Daddy told me and him to go inside and help Mom and Granny. I'm sure they appreciated the help.

At supper that night, Dad told us he was leaving the Model T for us to use and that he would be taking the early train Monday morning to the Junction and then Bangor & Aroostook RR to Bangor. He said he'd be going south to Brooks Field in San Antonio, Texas for his flight school.

Vernie wanted to know what a Texas was, so I told him it was another State. When he asked what a State was, I let Dad explain.

Early Monday morning we went down to the Station to watch Dad get on the train; well everybody but Granny and Marie did. Grandpa had to go to work, so he shook Daddy's hand and went to the engine house.

Daddy gave us all hugs and he kissed Mom and told her he would write. We all waved as Daddy stepped on board and Mr. Jackson the Conductor called all aboard.

I thought Mom had a tear in her eye as we turned and started back to the house. Just then Harold step out of the station and told us all good morning. He gave Mom a sympathetic hug, and told her it was going to be all right.

He said, "Billy, you'll have to take care of your Mom and brother and sister until your Dad gets back." Then he knelt down and stuck his hand out and said, "Deal?"

I shook his hand and said, "It's a deal, Harold."

Mom grinned, shook her head, looked at Harold and said, "You two." She took Vernie by one hand and me by the other and we headed back to Chapin Ave. and the walk to Granny's house.

I guess the mystery was solved, but I wasn't sure that me and Vernie knew the whole story yet.

That night after supper Granny pulled her scrapbook and asked if us young men would like to hear a story about the Railroad. Naturally we said yes.

MISHAPS FOR MONSON R.R.
April 20, 1922

"The past week has been a strenuous one for the Monson railroad. On the first trip to Monson Junction April 10 the engine left the rails near Day's crossing and plunged over the bank on to its side. One end of the passenger car was derailed but no one was injured.

The other engine was steamed up and went to the scene of the wreck with a crew. Not until Tuesday afternoon was the engine placed on the rails and towed back to the repair shop. Wednesday the first train out met with the same fate and very near the same place, this time the passenger car being torn from the trucks and tipped over. Mrs. A.L. Bray and little niece Edith Eastman and Conductor Morrill were the only occupants and were uninjured.

This wreck was cleared up Friday night and towed back to the repair shop. The trains Saturday got over the road without mishaps. Frost coming out was the cause of the wrecks. Mail and passengers were conveyed to and from the Junction."

A. Kronholm, J. Carlburg and Pearly Stevens

Granny said, "Clarence, tell the boys about those wrecks."

"What wreck, Granny?"

She slid the scrap book across the table and pointed to the pictured and said "This one."

"Oh yeah, I remember that day." Grandpa said. "If Pearly hadn't have been so quick on the brakes, it would have been a lot worse. You see, boys, in the spring when the ground begins to thaw, you never know where you are going find a soft spot. But nobody got hurt; still it took us until Friday night to clear up everything. Yep, I remember, she

101

went on her side on Monday, and we had the mess cleared up and were hauling mail and passengers by Saturday Morning."

He pushed the book back to Granny and went back to reading his Bible.

Granny read us a couple more articles from that same day's paper.

"The highways are the worst this spring for several years. Automobilist will have to wait a while longer before they can get over the roads outside the village.
Arthur Bray, our grocery man, officially opened the automobile season here Saturday by using his Ford truck about town."

EASTER AT THE BAPTIST CHURCH
Easter was appropriately observed at the Baptist Church Sunday, the church being filled at both services. In the morning the pastor preached on Easter Discoveries.

Mom came back downstairs, and told me and Vernie it was time for bed. I remember falling asleep thinking about planes and trains, and wondering when my Daddy would be back.

difficult railroading

August was a strange month in Maine; you never knew what the weather would do.

Vernie was complaining one morning that it sure was hot and that he wanted to go swimming over at Hebron Pond. Granny told him that we didn't have time to go up Hebron Pond, 'cause it would be hailing by the time we got there.

Grandpa said, "Vernie, if you don't like the weather wait ten minutes and it will change. Now finish your dinner."

"Pa?" I said, "Why do we call it dinner when it's in the middle of the day?"

"Granny, you explain it, I've got to get back up to the shop." Grandpa said as he got up from the table and went back to work.

"Boys, when you work as hard as your Daddy and Grandpa do, you need a big hearty breakfast to start the day. Come noontime, all of that food is used up and then you need a big hearty dinner so you have the strength to go back to work. Then after the day's labor is done, you can have supper.

It doesn't take as much energy to sleep as it does to work. Besides, that's what my Mother called it and that's good enough for me. Now finish eating, and go out and play, before it starts hailing."

We went out to play by the edge of Granny's truck farm. Vernie was right it was a hot summer day. Still, it seemed like the wind was picking up and the sky was getting darker.

I looked off to the west, and over the town the sky was a mass of black rolling clouds. They seemed to be racing towards me and Vernie. Suddenly I saw a brilliant flash, and the sky lit up. Then the thunder clapped so loud that me and Vernie covered our ears and ran for the house.

We barely made it before the ground was pelted with hail. I never did figure out how Granny knew what the weather was going to do. Guess that was another one of the mysteries of that summer in 1938.

I guess Mom felt like we needed to be entertained a bit, cause me and Vernie were starting to snarl at each other. So she set us down at the table and opened the scrapbook.

DIFFICULT RAILROADING
MARCH 18, 1918

"The past week has been the most severe of any for the winter. The Monson train was unable to get through to the Junction Wednesday as the engine that runs the snow plow was broken and was not repaired until late Thursday. Wednesday afternoon a team from A.S.Knight's stable managed to get through to the Junction and bring back the mail and a few passengers. Some of the passengers on the B.& A. train Wednesday night walked the six miles from the Junction to Monson, getting here about 10:30o'clock."

Stalled for the night

"The strongest wind of any day came Friday. The 5:50 train left on time with two engines and a passenger car but on reaching Day's crossing found more snow than it could plow through. After shoveling for some distance, it moved on to the vicinity of the S curve where it was stalled for the night. The passengers, seven or eight in number, were made as comfortable as possible and remained on the train until day break. The distance was not great to the junction and they walked it, taking the B. &A. for points west.

A crew of 10 or 12 men left here Saturday morning and went down the line to shovel out the worst drifts and the stalled train. About 2 P.M. Saturday afternoon the line was cleared and the train returned to Monson.

It has been a great many years since there was as much snow on the ground at this time of year. There are many drifts on the roads in the vicinity of this town that are from 10 to 15 feet deep."

Grandpa always told us that the Monson never had an accident that caused serious injury or death, and that proved to be true, but 1918 seem to be the year for major wrecks. While it wasn't necessarily unusual for a flat car loaded with slate to derail, if one of the locomotives came off the rails, the newspaper recorded it as a wreck.

WRECK ON THE MONSON RAILROAD
OCTOBER 28, 1918

A bad wreck occurred on the Monson railroad a few rods below the Portland-Monson siding Saturday afternoon about four when the engine left the rails and turned over on its side and three freight cars were derailed.

On its side but no one injured

The regular afternoon train left as usual for Monson Jct. hauled by No.4 engine, recently purchased new, in charge of Julius Carlberg, acting conductor, Wallace E. Howard, engineer, Irving Carlberg, fireman.

107

On reaching the Portland-Maine siding they stopped and took on two carloads of freight. The train was just getting under way then the accident occurred. Engineer Howard and Fireman Carlberg, also Kenneth Harmon a section hand were in the cab. When the engine left the rails Howard applied the brakes and before any in the cab had time to jump the engine went over on its side. Howard climbed out through the window on his side of the engine, while Carlberg and Harmon crawled from beneath the overturned machine, uninjured.

The road bed was torn up for several rods* and it took nearly all day Sunday to get the three derailed carloads of slate on to the irons and back to the siding. The work for getting the road bed rebuilt and the engine back on to the rails will take a day or two at least.

Passengers in the meantime will be conveyed to and from the Junction by automobiles. This is the first bad wreck on the mainline since the first years the railroad was built."

"I bet Granny was relieved that Grandpa wasn't the section hand that was on the train that day," I exclaimed.

When Mom read the part that said *"it took nearly all day Sunday…."* I knew why Grandpa was sometimes so tired he wasn't able to go to church and us kids.

108

Mom read some articles from October 29, 1918

"A collision occurred on Main Street near Henry Grover's store Saturday evening when G.L.Brown ran into Fred H. LaBrees' team with his automobile. Mr. Brown believes that had LaBree had a light on his wagon as the law requires he would avoided running into him."

Vernie thought it was funny that a horse and a car could have a wreck. I don't think he understood that the article was from almost 20 years ago.

*A 'Rod' is a unit of measurement used in surveying railroads. In modern US customary units it is defined as 16 1/2 US survey feet.

Chapter fourteen

troubled narrow gauge

As the month of August, 1938 wore on, I
could sense that something was going on.
For one thing I thought that my Daddy would be
home by now, but I guess his school took longer
that I thought.

For another, Grandpa was staying home from
work a lot. I had never known him to not go to
work, even when he was half sick. Still nobody in
the family seemed overly concerned, but I couldn't
shake the feeling that there was more to the story
than met the eye.

One afternoon, me and Vernie were playing out
front when we heard the train whistle as it was
crossing Chapin Ave. As soon as the locomotive
cleared the road, it slowed down and Grandpa
stepped off, shouted, "Thanks for the lift, Elwin,"
and started walking towards us.

We waved and then we took off towards him. Even though we weren't supposed to leave the yard. As he took Vernie's hand and we fell in step with him, I inquired worriedly, "You ain't sick are you, Pa, you're sure home early?"

"Nah, Billy, I'm just saving some work for tomorrow. Remember, I told you that I've never run out of work yet. Besides I thought of another story about the Monson I wanted to tell you boys, and I was afraid if I didn't get home and get started I'd forget."

So the three of us climbed up the front porch steps, and went in side.

"Granny," Grandpa said, "If we say please could you bring me and these young men a snack and something to drink? We're gonna be on the porch swing, swapping yarns."

Vernie said he didn't want to knit, he wanted a story.

Patiently, Grandpa said, "Vernie, a yarn is just another name for a story, so you just hold your horses for a minute."

About that time Granny came out with that big old, yellow mixing bowl of hers, heaping full of pop corn and Mom was right behind her with three glasses of lemonade. I swear, that bowl was big enough that Marie could almost take bath in it.

"Think this will hold you boys till supper?" Granny inquired.

Grandpa said we'd better move to the steps or we'd be wearing lemonade and popcorn. So we moved to the steps, Vernie in the middle and me and Grandpa on each side. Vernie had to sit one step higher than me and Grandpa, so Grandpa put the bowl on the step in front of Vernie where we could all reach it.

Heavy snow troubles the Narrow Gauge Railroad

We each grabbed a handful of popcorn and Grandpa started on his yarn: "I'm pretty sure, no, I'm positive, it in was in March of 1912. We'd had as much rough weather as we had seen during the whole winter thus far. The week beginning on the fourth started pretty mild but by afternoon

113

things changed. The next day, Tuesday was the worst day by far that winter, snow beginning to fall early Monday evening and it continued the remainder of the night and nearly all day Tuesday; must have been 18 or 20 inches by nightfall."

"How many is 18 or 20 Inches, Pa?" Vernie wondered.

"Vernie, the top of the snow was as high as this porch floor, and that's a lot of snow." He paused for another bite of popcorn and then continued, "The railroad was affected the worst it has been for many a year. About eight inches of snow had fallen by the time the 5:45 a.m. train left for Monson Junction. In less than one-half mile from the station the train got stuck. Well, Pearly was the engineer on that run and he transferred the two passengers to the locomotive and uncoupled the car. They left the car behind and finally made it to the Junction, but they missed the connection with the train coming down from Greenville."

"What did they do with the passenger car?" It was my turn to interrupt.

"Let me get this straight in my mind now. It's been a few years since 1912 you know. Seems to me it took about an hour-and-a-half to get things shoveled out so the train could start back to the village. Everything went fairly well for about three miles when they were obliged to stop on account

114

of the snow pilling up on the plow so high that the plow would not throw the snow out. From there to nearly the station they were forced to shovel."

Before either of us could ask, Grandpa said, "As I recall they shoveled about two miles. When they finally got back to the passenger car, they pushed it to the station. Now the train was supposed to be back in Monson at 7:00 o'clock that morning, but it didn't get through until 5:30 that night, it was ten-and-one-half hours late."

"Gosh, Pa, that's almost a whole day," I said around a mouthful of popcorn. "What happened next?"

"Harold said that in all his experience railroading, that was the worst snow he ever saw to plow through. I reckon that if anybody knew, it would be Harold; he's been with the railroad almost since its beginning.

We, that is the section men, turned the plow on the table, hooked up both engines and the passenger car and about six or a little after we headed back to the Junction. We got through all right, but we didn't get back with the mail until after eight o'clock that night.

Unfortunately, about 35 or 40 passengers had to spend the night at the Junction with nothing but oranges and bananas to eat."

"Really, Pa, nothing but oranges and bananas?"

"You can just ask Granny to show you the newspaper clipping after supper"

That pretty much settled it. I think he thought we wouldn't think to ask Granny, but we did, before the supper dishes were done.

SNOWSTORM TROUBLES NARROW GAUGE ROAD

March 4, 1912

Unfortunately for 35 or 40 members of Onaway lodge, No. 106, I.O.O.F., who went to Greenville the day before, where they held a meeting in the hall at that place, they had to either spend the day at Monson Junction or "hike" it home, six miles away. Judging from the reports of some of the unfortunate ones Monson Junction is a very exciting railroad center. A crate of oranges and some bananas helped to appease the hunger of the excursionists.

As night drew near teams were telephoned for to come and get those who had not started on foot, as rather poor quarters were offered for a night's lodging provided the train did not get through.

About four o'clock that afternoon two teams of four horses each left for the Junction and about eight that night returned with most of the Odd Fellows.

The excitement of the story was over, and my mind returned to my concern about Grandpa coming home from work so early. My world just seemed to be out of balance, so when Mom was tucking us in bed that night, in a whisper so I wouldn't wake Marie I asked Mom.

"Is Pa alright, Mommy? He's not sick is he?"

"Now, Billy why would you think that?"

"He sure came home from work early, not that I don't want him home, especially with Daddy gone, but ..."

"Well, Billy, the truth is the slate business is slowing down, and the Monson Slate Company owns the railroad, so the railroad doesn't have as much work as it used to. Grandpa can't stay and work if there's no work for him to do."

"So he's not sick, then?"

"No, he's okay, now you go to sleep." She gave a kiss on the forehead and turned off the light.

I guess Grandpa was okay, but I forgot to ask about Daddy.

Chapter fifteen

changes

We were headed toward the end of August, the 28th, would be my tenth birthday. I didn't think I'd ever make it. I knew better than to expect anything, but I was hoping for a spice cake without raisins.

It was Saturday night, and Granny had drug that big old galvanized wash tub into the kitchen and filled it with nice warm water. Marie always got the first bath, cause she was a girl, then Vernie was next. Granny added a little more hot water to warm things up a bit when it was his turn.

Being the oldest and the biggest, I always was last, but Mom let me wash myself, except for my hair and my ears; she still did that. Granny kept a kettle of warm water heating for Mom to rinse my hair with. As Mom was rinsing my hair and I was sputtering and spitting, she asked me if I knew of any special things coming up.

I told her my birthday was coming soon; I could tell because I saw it on Granny's calendar.

"That's right Billy. Only one more day and you be ten years old.

"But, Mommy, why does Granny have the first of September circled too?"

"It's getting close to bedtime. How about I let Grandpa tell you in the morning. Granny's making chicken and dumplings for dinner, and right after church we're going to have a little party. And maybe we'll have little surprise for you. Okay?"

"Okay, Mommy." And that was that.

Billy and Vernon around 1938

The next morning me and Vernie dressed in our best overalls, and we all went to church. Marie and Vernie both fell asleep during the preaching, but I was too excited to think of anything except chicken and dumplings and my surprise.

None of the adults said anything about it being my birthday that morning before church. I hope they hadn't forgot.

When church was done, we all pilled back into the model T and Grandpa drove us home.

"You boys go upstairs and change out of your good clothes," Mom directed. "And hurry back down and, Billy, you can help set the table."

"I want to help too, Mommy." Vernie cried.

"Yes, Vernie, you can put the silverware on."

As we were finishing up dinner Grandpa said "Seems like there was something I wanted to talk with you about, Billy, or maybe it was something I was going to say."

I was practically hanging off the edge of my chair waiting to hear.

"Doggone if I can remember. Granny, do you remember what I wanted to say to Billy?"

Granny looked at Mom, Mom looked at Grandpa, and at the same time they all started singing "Happy Birthday" to me.

I knew they wouldn't forget.

Mom and Granny cleared the table, and Mom came out carrying a big spice cake, and Granny brought some canned peaches to go with it.

I knew better than to expect a present, but I was still waiting to hear what was so special about September first. And I was sorta hanging on to hope for a surprise.

Granny came in from the kitchen and said, "looks like a good afternoon to stay inside. The wind is picking and the air has got that feeling of rain, and so does my knee."

"Well, in that case, I think I'll just prop my feet up on the ottoman and take a little Sunday afternoon nap." Grandpa said as he was leaning back in his chair.

"But, Pa?"

"What is it now, Billy?"

"I thought you were going tell us a story about the railroad or something."

"What do you mean, *or something*?"

"Uh, well, I was wondering why, uh, why September first is circled on Granny's calendar?"

He sat up, put his hands on his knees, and leaned over to look at me and said, "Oh is that what *or something* is?"

"Well, Billy, it's 1938 and lots of things in the world are changing, and many of those changes are going to affect us. The first one that is going to affect us happens on September first." And he started to lean back like that was all he was going to say.

By this time Vernie was pretty interested too, and we chimed in together "But what's going happen, Pa?"

"Now you boys know Harold? Well, of course you do. Well, Harold turned 74 years old last May, and he's decided that 54 years is long enough to work, so he's going to retire. I was only four years old when Harold started as a fireman on the Monson Railroad that's just about the same age as Marie is now."

Vernie wanted to know what "Retire" was. So did I, but I wasn't going to ask.

"That means he doesn't have to go to work anymore, Vernie"

"What's gonna happen to his railroad, Pa?"

"Everything will stay the same for right now, except Paul—you know Paul Jackson the clerk? He is going to be the new superintendent. Harold's last day will be December eighth, he just hanging around to help Paul get a handle on things."

There was a clap of thunder, and the house shook, and the hail started pounding on the roof so hard that we couldn't hear ourselves think. It must have lasted ten or fifteen minutes, then that squall passed and it settled in to rain for the duration of the day.

When things got quiet, Grandpa inquired, "I've been thinking, would you boys like to hear a short railroad story"

"This ain't a trick is it, Pa?"

"No, it's the truth. I'm sure you can remember me telling you about all the break-downs we had with engines Number 1 and 2. Remember one time they both broke piston rods at the same time, and I told you about how Harold disconnected the broken rod from each engine. Anyway, he managed to hook the two broken engines together so we could get the train through.

"Well, I want to tell you about the day we got Number 3.

"Way back in November of 1912, Harold convinced the board of directors-that's the men that are his bosses."

"Harold had a boss?"

"Yes, Billy, even bosses have bosses. But anyway, he convinced his boss that it would be cheaper to buy a new locomotive, than it would be to keep fixing Number 2. So he ordered a new Vulcan and it arrived in February 20, 1913. Granny, where's that picture Harold gave all the employees when Number 3 arrived?"

"It's in the top drawer of the bureau, Clarence, I keep meaning to put it in the scrapbook."

Grandpa started to get up, but Mom said she'd get it for him.

Vulcan Builder's Photo Monson Number 3

"Wasn't she a beauty?" Grandpa asked as he showed us the photo.

"Boy, she don't look like that now, Pa."

"I reckon she's showing her twenty-years alright."

"Billy"

"Yes, Mom."

"I have a little surprise for you and Vernie, come here and sit down on the davenport with me and I'll tell you about it before supper"

At the word surprise me and Vernie were all ears. We sat down one on each side, and Mom held Marie on her lap.

She pulled a letter out of an envelope and started to read.

"Dearest family,

I have completed my school now, and I am now working to become a full time flight instructor. The Aircorp thinks because of my age—I'm considered old at 29—I can make the biggest contribution by teaching. So they promoted me to a Captain US Army Aircorp.

I hope you get this letter in time for Billy's tenth Birthday, I know he's growing into a fine young man.

I will be getting a furlough soon and then I'll be home for a visit. I can't wait to see you all.

Love, Daddy.

PS here's some money to help out."

"Dad, Mom, would you look at this!" Mom exclaimed. "He send us $125.00!"

Chapter sixteen

Chores

B illy." I heard a voice faintly through the fog.

"Billy." I heard it again stronger this time.

"Billy." It's Mom, I thought. I must be late for Church.

"Billy!" Louder.

"I'm awake, Mommy"

"Bill, what's the matter with you?"

Huh, that didn't sound like Mommy.

"Bill, are you going to play trains all day?" Hattie called from the railroad room door. "Oh, I get it!, You've been napping. Wake up, Goofy." She called me Goofy a lot, said that's what my middle initial G. was for.

I felt her shake me and give me a big sloppy kiss right across my face. I opened my eyes and Bella was licking my cheek and trying to crawl up on my lap.

"Oh hi, sweetheart; I guess I dozed off."

"Yeah, you must have dozed off, alright; do I look like your Mommy?" Hattie said, as she put her hand on her hip and gave a little shake.

Sometimes that woman thinks we're still a couple of kids. Besides I couldn't reach her from where I was sitting, anyway.

"Come in the house and have some lunch, and then you can do your chores."

"What chores? I did everything this morning."

"Oh yeah. Well, I managed to dig up a few more." Hattie replied with a sly grin.

What'd I tell you about being retired?

I didn't have a clue about what I could have forgotten. I'd helped with breakfast dishes, carried out the trash and the ashes. It was recycle pick-up day (if the truck could get through), so I hauled all of the recycle out. I'd split extra kindling, filled the wood box and the wagon. I had carried her sewing machine so she wouldn't have too, and I'd moved Granny's scrap book out of her way. I didn't want to overdo it. I remembered Grandpa White telling me to save some work for later so I didn't run out.

Well, I had to admit; I was a little hungry after thinking about all that work I had done. And actually, I was feeling like Joey. I could eat a horse or something.

When I passed through the living room, I glanced at the clock on the wall, and it said 12:45. Actually it didn't say anything, but the hands were pointing to the "12" and the "9" which is 12:45. If you don't understand it; just take my word for. I'm too old to teach anyone how to read an analog clock. I'd tried once with Joey and ended up buying him a digital watch. That was easier and a lot quicker.

A look out the window told me the skies were clear. Bright sunshine was reflecting off the snow cover on the mountain across the lake. The water was sparkling, and the breeze was gentle. The temperature was up to 37. I could see the road below the house, and could tell that the county plows had been through. Snow was melting and dripping off the roof.

Maybe, I'd been asleep for days instead of an hour or so. It was like the whole world had changed from this morning. I remembered Grandpa White saying, "If you don't like the weather, wait five minutes and it'll change." Seems like he was right.

Well, I thought to myself, I'll just bet that Hattie wants to go the town, and I am going to have to shovel the driveway enough for her get the truck out.

I kept my bet to myself, as I sat down at the table to eat. As I reached across to hold Hattie's hand and ask the Blessing, she said, "It's only a light lunch, tomato soup and grilled cheese; I'll make a big supper when I get back from town."

(Don't mean to tell you I told you so, but I told you so.)

"Oh, I didn't know you were going to town," I replied innocently.

"Well, I didn't either, but it turned out to be such a pretty day. Besides, I need a couple things to finish the quilt I'm making for Mya's birthday. Anyway, eat and then you can go out and clear the snow off the truck and shovel the drifts away so I can get out."

Bella took full advantage of the opportunity to play in the snow for a half hour. I'm sure she enjoyed it more than I did. I started the truck to defrost the windshield, and right on schedule, Hattie came out the door, gave me a kiss and climbed in the nice warm four-wheel-drive truck.

As she closed the door and as she was buckling up, she rolled down the window, "Oh, by the way, I'm stopping by Nancy's if the roads are clear. Do you need anything?"

"Chocolate" was my one word answer.

I watched her drive off. Bella and I brushed the snow off and went inside. I turned on the coffee pot, filled my cup with hot water to temper it, and ran out to the railroad room for Granny's scrapbook. Bella was on my heels the whole way. I poured my coffee, figured the extra chores had earned me a cookie or two so I grabbed a couple on the way out of the kitchen.

We figured-Bella and I that is-that we had a couple of hours to ourselves, so I gave Bella a doggie cookie and bit into one myself. I promptly spit it out of my mouth and gave the rest to Bella; seems I was a little distracted and bit into the wrong cookie.

Oh well, that wasn't the first mistake I'd made; I washed the taste out of my mouth with a swallow of coffee, took a bite of a fresh cookie and opened the scrapbook.

April 4, 1927
"Another serious accident occurred in the slate quarries of this town Wednesday, March 30, when Ernest Sandberg, a workman in the pit at the Monson Pond quarry lost his right arm at the elbow. Mr. Sandberg was at work in the tunnel when a rock weighing several tons fell from the

overhead only a short distance and severed his arm, then rolled a short distance and pinned him where he lay. Fellow workmen came to his assistance immediately and did all possible.

He was taken to Monson Junction by train and to Guilford on a gasoline hand car. At Guilford he was taken to the Chase hospital where he was made as comfortable as possible. His condition is serious but attending physicians have hopes of recovery.

Mr. Sandberg is a man about 35 years old and has followed the quarry work for nearly 20 years. His many friends hope for a speedy recovery and extend their greatest sympathy to his wife and child, parents and brothers.

For some reason, a lot of the articles in Piscataquis Observer, seemed to deal with difficulties of some kind. Guess it was a lot like the things that make the news today, the bad things.

I think a hundred years ago, life was a lot harder than it is today, and life a hundred years from now will probably be a lot easier than it is today.

Still I think human nature has always been and always will be the same. Like Grandpa used to say about the weather: it's a Hebrews 13:8 day:

(Jesus Christ) the same yesterday and today and forever.

Chapter seventeen

joey's back

Bella and me were napping and the telephone rang and woke us up. I got up to answer it and it was Nancy.

"Hi, Mom home?"

"No, she went to town, and then she was coming to your house if the road is open."

"Well she's not here."

"Nancy, she's not here either."

"Okay bye." click

I hung up and went to sit back down, but before I could the phone rings again. It's Hattie this time.

"I been trying to call Nan to tell her I coming over, but her line has been busy"

"Hattie, she already knows you are planning to stop by."

"How does she know that?"

"I just told her."

"What'd you do call her?"

"No, she called here, I was having a perfectly good nap, too."

"Well what did she want?"

"Sweetheart, she wanted to talk to you, when I told her you weren't home she said 'okay bye' and hung up."

"Okay, bye." click.

Sometimes I feel like I live in the state of confusion, I think it borders on insanity.

I was certainly wide awake now; might as well throw some wood in the fire and see if I can find another cup of coffee. Then I got to wondering and thinking how quickly things change. It didn't seem that long ago that having your own telephone was a big deal.

When we first got married, we had to go up to the store or to a neighbor's house to make a call. Then when we did get a phone we had to listen for a special ring—you know like 'ring-ring-riiiiiiing-ring'. Everybody had their own special ring that they were supposed to hear before they were to answer; we had what was called a "Party Line."

But sometimes people would answer every ring just so they could listen into somebody else's conversation Of course if you caught them listening, they's just say sorry and hang up.

Maybe that's why it's called a party line, it was sort of like a parlor game or something. To make a call you had to pick up the phone and if none of the other people on your party line were using the phone you would hear the dial tone and you could make your call. If somebody was on the phone you just quietly said, 'excuse me', and hung up.

The last rule was that you weren't supposed to have real long conversations.

I remember one time I needed to make a real important call and every time I picked up the phone, it was busy. Now, I don't remember what was so important about my phone call, but I do remember that day. I'd been trying for over half-an-hour to make my call.

Mae Anderson was talking with Mrs. Brown. They were our neighbors, one on each side of us. I'd put the phone down and wait a few minutes and try again. Finally after all that time, I heard Mrs. Brown say she had a big pot of beans simmering on the stove. I very quietly hung up again. Five more minutes went by and I decided to try again.

When I picked up the phone the ladies were still talking. I took a deep breath and with panic in my voice said, "OH MY LORD, I smell beans burning!"

Suddenly Mrs. Brown yelled,"Mae, I've got to run! My beans are burning up!" and she hung up.

I'm not sure I understand why, but suddenly I was able to get my call through.

Now days, rich people have these things called "cell phones." They've got them in their cars and they can carry them around like a big purse with a phone sticking out of the top.

I saw an article in Popular Mechanics that said if they could make the batteries smaller, some day everyone could have their own private cell phone.

I thought when Armstrong landed on the moon I'd seen everything, but I was wrong. I'll bet my Granny was just as amazed at the progress that she witnessed during her lifetime, as I have been in mine.

Think about it for a minute. When Granny was born in December of 1882, nobody had cars, there were no airplanes, no indoor plumbing.

Here we are in 1999 and people have cars, and computers, microwaves, and we worry about this thing called Y2K.

Anyway, back to Granny's scrapbook. I figured I'd have plenty of time to read, since Hattie and Nancy were together. I'd be lucky if I had to eat left overs. No seriously, I mean it, I'd be lucky to have left over anything that Hattie had cooked, it would sure beat my cooking.

OCTOBER 29, 1918

"As there had been no cases of influenza in town, the churches were opened Sunday and the schools were to have reopened Monday, but several suspicious cases were reported Sunday afternoon and the ban was once more placed on all public places."

I shudder when I think about what my parents and grandparents lived through. The 1918 flu pandemic took the lives of over 600,000 people. I have no Idea how many people didn't survive the depression. Sure makes me grateful for what Hattie and me and our kids have today.

Can you even imagine what the world must have been like in 1918 during the influenza pandemic: people all over the world dying? Families quarantined in their homes, not able to visit relatives, schools closed, churches closed. I read that the pandemic lasted until sometime in 1920 before things began to get back to normal.

I had just about decided that I'd go see what was in the refrigerator, when I heard the truck pull up. Bella heard it too; I could tell by her bark. People think dogs can't talk. Ha, I can tell from Bella's bark when she's hungry or happy or wants out.

I set Granny's book on the end table and lowered the foot rest of my recliner and stood up just as Hattie came through the door.

"You can just sit back down, Billy. Joey just came to visit and he's already helped unload. I don't have enough stuff that I need your help with it too."

I said, "I'll help any way, sweetheart, I'd hate to waste all that energy I just used by standing up."

"Well, if you've got that much energy, you can go out and shovel the walk off."

"I didn't say I had a lot of energy; I just said I didn't want to waste any," I replied as I put on boots and headed out the door. Bella took one look at me pulling my coat and gloves on and lay back down and closed her eyes.

Joey smiled at me over the bag of groceries he was carrying and went inside.

Guess I was on my own this time.

Chapter eighteen

the last whistle

H ard to believe that only a week had gone by since Joey's last visit. In my mind, I'd relived more than sixty years since he was here. I was still thinking about the year I'd turned 10 years old, the summer of 1938.

"Joey, would you like to hear the story of 1938, the year I turned ten years old?"

"I sure would."

"That was the summer my Dad, your Great -grandfather, moved all of us kids up to Monson to stay with Granny and Grandpa White while he was in Texas. My dad had always wanted to fly. As a matter of fact, he had soloed before him and my mom got married."

"So is that why you learned too, Grandpa?"

"Yes, Joe, but that's another story for another day, okay?"

"Okay"

"I didn't know it at the time but things were really tough, money-wise, even though my Dad was lucky and kept his job all though the depression. Then my Dad saw an advertisement in the <u>Bangor Daily News </u>for Army pilots, and the pay was better than being a mechanic. So my dad joined up, but because of his age—he was 29 in 1938—and the fact that he had already learned to fly before he joined, the Army made him a flight instructor.

So he was able to send money home to mom to help take care of everybody. The Monson Railroad was really not doing very well. The slate business was dropping off, trucks were taking a lot of the freight that the railroad used to handle, especially in the summer when the road to Abbot was better. The railroading was better in the summer too, but that didn't seem to make much difference.

Mr. Morrill, who had done every job there was to do on the railroad, retired. Then the next year, 1939 the railroad stopped all passenger trains. My grandpa only got called in to work if they were short-handed or stuck in the snow.

Grandpa would cut firewood for people, using Dad's old model T and trailer to haul it in. And since I was pretty stout, just like you are, Joey, I'd go help. Granny and Mom still worked in Granny's truck farm, sometimes selling vegetables.

Dad came home on a furlough for two weeks in the spring of 1939, and it was really great to see him. So between the money Dad sent every month, and the firewood and vegetables, we had it better than a lot of people.

Mom and Dad were making plans for all of us to join him in Texas, but by then war was breaking out in Europe. Then the Japanese bombed Pearl Harbor on December the 7th, 1941, and America joined the War.

We worried for a while that Dad would have to go overseas, but the Army Aircorp wanted him to stay and teach multi-engine pilots. At least he didn't go overseas, but we didn't see him, except once more in 1943, until the war was over."

"Gosh, Grandpa, I sure didn't know all of that."

"Well, Joey, let's see what your Grandma's got for supper."

The weather stayed pretty good, the snow was quickly melting, and the days were getting longer. Joey and I went out after supper and filled up the wagon and the wood box. Even though the days were longer, the early mornings and evenings were still cold, and it was nice to have a little fire to take the chill off.

Joey wanted to pull the wagon load of wood to the wood box. I didn't think he could it, but like I said, he was pretty stout for a ten-year old, and he handled it just fine.

We had some free time and we knew it would be a while until Hattie was ready to fix us some dessert, so Joey asked me if we could run the trains for a bit.

He didn't have to twist my arm. Besides I was ready for him. I figured he'd ask for a Monson railroad story. And he did, just about the time I got settled on to my railroad stool, where I could run a train too.

"You got any more Monson Railroad stories that Grandpa White told you?"

"No, Joey, sorry. I guess I'm all out of Grandpa White's railroad stories."

"Really? You can't remember any?"

"Nope, not a one." I said as grin began to form on my face, "But, I got a story I can tell you about the Monson Railroad that I saw with my own eyes. 'Course, you probably don't want to hear that kind of story, do you?"

"Oh yes I do, Grandpa, please."

"It's a real sad story Joey, real sad, are you sure?"

"I can handle it, go ahead."

"Okay, but don't blame me if it makes you cry."

"Grandpa, I won't cry."

"Well, it was the last part of November, 1943, the War was going on in the south Pacific Ocean and in Europe. It was truly a World War. America had just got through the depression; now our Government was rationing everything: sugar, gasoline, rubber, all kinds of things. Everything that could be used in the war was. Mom and Granny were even saving tin cans and turning them in at a collection center.

Me and Grandpa White were cutting pulp wood and selling to the mills as fast as we could, any body who could cut pulp wood did. It was real important for the war effort."

"What's so important about pulp wood?" Joey wondered out loud.

"The pulp was turned into all kinds of things: explosives and gas mask filters, blueprint papers for planning ships and planes, strong paper wrappings for food shipments to our troops abroad. Pulp wood still has many uses today.

Anyway, young men were joining the army and navy to go fight the Nazis and women were taking jobs in factories to help the war effort. The railroads were moving people and supplies all over the county. At least all the big railroads were; the Monson was still struggling.

I wanted to join up to be a pilot, but I was only 15 and my Mom wouldn't sign for me and I knew better than to lie about my age. So I helped in other ways.

On Nov. 22nd and 23rd, 1943, we had 16-inches of snow and the electric power was out from Monday until Friday night. Somehow the local telephone service was not interrupted, but nobody could make calls out of town.

None of the side streets in town got plowed; neither did the road to Blanchard, Elliotsville and Williamantic. They didn't get plowed until the following week."

"What's that got to do with the Monson Railroad?"

"Joe, hold on. I'm getting there. I have to tell it in order, or I might leave something out."

"Well, could you get to the exciting part?"

"There ain't no exciting part, only a sad part. Anyway on Monday morning, November the 28th, in the early morning just as the sun was coming up, the piercing sound of a steam locomotive whistle echoed in the cloudy morning sky.

Vernie and me ran outside to see what was going on. Vernie was the same age as you are, Joey, ten-years-old. We ran toward the station, as the whistle sounded again. When we got to the station, the engine was pulling an empty flat car, and backing down towards the quarry.

There was a crowd of people gathering at the station. Everybody was surprised to see the little narrow-gauge train running again. Paul Jackson,

The wrecking train

the superintendent, was standing on the station platform with Harold Morrill.

As we ran up, Harold said good morning to us; we told him good morning. Then I asked, 'What's going on Harold? Is the railroad running again?'

'No, Billy, I'm sad to say all of the metal has been sold to the Rochester Iron and Metal Company from Rochester, New York. This train today is the wrecking train. It will haul all of the rail that is being pulled up to the Junction to be transferred to the B. & A. train.

Unfortunately, your Grandpa is helping to take up the rail, and it's a sad job for him, because I

145

know he loves this little narrow gauge as much as Paul and I do. Right, Paul?'

Yes, Harold, it's a sad day, but our little six-mile -long railroad can help more with the war effort by being melted down, used to make planes and ships than it can by hauling materials.' "

I paused for minute, to let Joey digest what I had just said. I must admit, however, that my pause was also to let me get control of my emotions and not cry again when I remembered that sad day.

"What about the locomotives, Grandpa?" Joey wanted to know.

"Well, Joe, I'll tell you exactly what the newspaper said" and I reached for Granny's scrap book.

Monson #3 and 4 loaded for shipment

"Thus when the last rail is removed the engines will be loaded for shipment and the little narrow railroad and train which has run for more than 50 years will be a thing of the past,"

I glanced at Joey, and he was turning away from me to dry his eyes. I quickly wiped my own and tried to change the subject.

"Hey, Joe, let's go see what's for desert."

proved its worth

B efore we barely got up from the breakfast table the next morning, Joey already had a day's worth of questions lined up.

"Grandpa, why was the Monson only six miles long?"

"Well, Joe, that's because...."

"And since it was so short, why did they build it in the first place?"

"Hold on just a minute......"

"Why did they call it the 'peanut roaster'

"Whoa, Joe, slow down and take breath and I'll tell you the whole story. You sit back at the table and I'll be right back. Let me get another cup of coffee."

"I think I want to hear this too," Hatti said as she poured Joey another cup of chocolate and joined us at the table. "I might even have a couple of questions myself, or I might have to help you answer Joey's questions since you probably can't remember the answers."

"You both can sit there and be still. I'll get one of my books and we'll see who knows the answers."

Hatti leaned over and whispered something to Joe as I was sitting back down.

"Okay, here we go," I said as I opened the book. There was no way I was gonna let Hatti get the best of me this time.

"Because the slate underlying the town of Monson," I began, "had a very low ionizable mineral content, it was well suited for making electric switchboard, sinks, bath tubs, tabletops, chalk boards, roof shingles and head stones."

"What's ionizable?" Joey and Hatti chimed in together.

"I think it means that it won't conduct electricity, but you better ask your teacher, Joe." I replied, "Hatti, if you can find our dictionary, we'll look it up later. Well, transporting these heavy products was difficult in good weather and nearly impossible when spring thaw turned roads to slush. In 1882 the Bangor and Piscatquis Railroad by-passed Monson by a distance of six miles; thus the need for a short-line railroad was established. Did you get that? The standard gauge missed Monson by six miles."

"We got it." Hatti sighed.

I got the feeling my answers to Joe's questions were taking a little longer than she expected.

"So, the Monson and Athens Railroad Company was chartered in November, 1882. The primary purpose of the Monson, was to service the several slate mines and finishing houses in Monson. Maine. It was a two-foot, narrow-gauge railroad. It operated between the town of Monson and Monson Junction a stop on the Bangor and Aroostook Railroad, near Abbot, Maine, a distance of only six miles.

"According to the May 17, 1890 edition of The Scientific American it was the smallest railroad in the United States. It was the longest lasting above ground two-foot gauge common carrier railroad in the US. (The Chicago Tunnel Company continued to operate as a common carrier underground two-foot-gauge railroad until 1959)

"The first train arrived at Monson Station on September 4, 1883; on October 15, the railroad opened for business with two round trip trains scheduled daily. The name was changed to the Monson Railroad in 1885."

I looked up from my dissertation, and Hatti took the opportunity to excuse herself.

"Looks like you boys have got this under control and I've got Mya's birthday present to finish, come on LC."

LC got up, stretched, and followed Hatti to the bedroom.

I continued, "In 1908 the Monson Maine Slate Company gained control of the railroad, and the following year an extension was built to the Eighteen Quarry. At one time the Monson Railroad was serving eight quarries as well as the local saw and grist mills.

"The railroad replaced its original engines, buying Number 3 in 1920 at a cost of $2250.00 and Number 4 in 1917. It operated with link and pin couplers and stub turnouts for its entire life.

"After the last of the rails were taken up in 1944, in 1945 Francis Marshall purchased the company and continued to haul freight by truck until 1958. The Monson Maine Slate Company Railroad was officially dissolved in 1975.

"The little "Peanut Roaster" locomotives never turned around. They ran forward to the Junction and backward to Monson. Sometimes the Engine would be in the middle of the train, pushing some cars and pulling others at the same time.

"Does that answer you questions, Joey?"

"Sure does Grandpa, but what happened to the all the flatcars and box cars after the engines were hauled away?"

"Joey, I was told that all of the wooden rolling stock was burned and the metal parts recovered and sold for salvage. It was a sad sight to see the two little locomotives loaded on Bangor and

Aroostook flatcars destined for Rochester, New York, and the scrappers torch.

"In 1946, by some twist of fate, Linwood Moody found Monson Locomotives #3 and #4 in the Rochester scrap yard, neither of them having been cutup. Moody notified Ellis D. Atwood of the Edaville Railroad, and both locomotives were saved and are still in operation in Wiscasset, Maine.

"Neither my Grandpa White, nor Harold Morrill, were alive to learn of the fate of the two locomotives, they both loved so much. I didn't learn of both locomotives surviving until many years latter."

"Thanks Grandpa." He shouted as he ran out the door to meet his mom.

I'm not sure how or why I ended up with Granny White's scrap book, but I did, and I have enjoyed having it many times over the years. I suppose someday when Hattie can't find any more chores for me to do, and I've run out of all that work I been saving, I'll sit down and paste all off the loose articles like this one in place.

April 15, 1912

"A party made up of Miss Lucile Bray, Miss Sarah Bray, Miss Blandine Strout, Miss Marguerite Jackson, Miss Gladys Glover, Miss Beatrice Morrill

and Miss Maida Ham had a pleasant trip to the sap birth of Leslie Hescock in Abbot Saturday Morning. The young ladies took the early train, got off at Ladd brook and went the rest of the way on the crust. This was the first time they had ever visited such a place and they enjoyed it very much."

It's hard for me to imagine a common carrier railroad today, stopping on the main line to let a group of girls off the train for a pleasant walk along a brook.

Many times I've recalled that last sentence in the <u>Portland Sunday Telegram</u> article that said "many times the little railroad has proved its worth in an emergency."

It seems to me that it didn't have to be an emergency for the Monson Railroad to "prove its worth."

Chapter twenty

ripples

The closer it got to the spring equinox, the more confused the weather became. At least that's the way it looked to me. These past several days, we'd had just about everything you'd ever want; rain, hail, thunder, lightning, snow, wind and for the last two days sunshine.

I'm talking sunshine, you know when the sky is so bright and clear it almost hurts your eyes, and the birds are chirping and singing so loud it almost hurts your ears. Our big old cherry tree out front was full of pink blossoms and singing birds.

Perfect weather for staying inside, at least in my opinion. Of course Hatti couldn't wait for me to get out and take care of some of that work I'd been saving up. I tried to tell her it wouldn't spoil if I went past the 'finish-by date', and she didn't have to worry about anybody else coming and doing before I could get to it.

I stood up and stretched, pulled open the drapes and looked out across the lake; it looked like a sheet of glass. Just then, I saw a fish jump and make a big splash and the ripples started out in a circle across the lake. The circle of ripples was getting larger and larger and weaker and weaker, but still affecting the calm surface of the water. The ripple continued until it had lost all of its strength, was finished disturbing the calm, and then the waters settled back down.

One little fish, one big splash, and the calm surface of the entire lake was disturbed.

Part of that ripple actually reached the shore of the lake and reversed its direction. It met the incoming ripples, and when it did it became even larger. Part of the circle seemed to die harmlessly in the middle of the lake, but I wondered; does the ripple disturb things below the surface too.

Then it occurred to me: lots of things can cause ripples, not just in the water of the lake, but in the waters of life as well.

The weather? Doesn't the weather cause a ripple effect across our lives. It certainly had an effect on the Monson Railroad, and the whole village as well.

But I'm not talking about ripples started by something we can't control. I talking about those little pebbles that we toss into the pond of life that ripple out across the whole pond. You know what I mean, like what we say to someone else in anger, by our rude actions or reactions to others; or a snide remark.

Here it is many years later and I still remember meeting Harold Morrill for the first time. His kindness to me that day still ripples through my life. This was a man who was very important in his community, certainly a powerful man in many ways; yet he came down to my level and took away my fears.

Mr. Morrill touched me in a positive way, clear back in 1934. He taught me to try to see things from the other guy's position. He knew I was a terrified kid, so instead of glaring down at me, he came down to my level in a gentle way.

I haven't always succeeded in following his example, but I've tried to and always meant to.

In life we never see the whole effect of the ripple. We never know the whole story, or how what we said or did could ripple out and affect someone in a positive or negative way.

I guess what got me thinking along these lines was Granny's scrapbook; that shouldn't surprise you. Anyway, she had saved Mr. Morrill's obituary.

Harold E. Morrill,
Monson was Highly Esteemed

"Mr. Morrill was born in Brownville on May 27, 1864. Around 1876, the family moved to Monson, were he attended public schools and graduated from Monson Academy. At the age of 20 he went to work for the Monson Railroad as a fireman on the engine. Two years later he became engineer which position he held until late summer in 1904, when he was promoted to superintendent of the company.... He held this office until his retirement on December 1st, 1938, thus serving the Monson Railroad Company a total of 54 years.

He was naturally mechanically inclined and all through the years did much of the repair work on the rolling stock of the road himself. He studied telegraphy after becoming an employee of the company and in 1887 became the official telegraph operator and handled that branch of the service up to his retirement. In 1918 the company took over [operations of] the American Express Agency and he became the agent for the remaining years in their service.

During his years of railroading he was fireman, engineer, brakeman, conductor, freight agent, express agent, ticket agent, telegraph operator, train dispatcher, in fact every official that goes with railroading. Mr. Morrill was very efficient and faithful in all his 54 years of service and his retirement was deeply regretted by all who did business with the road."

Harold E. Morrill in his Engineer hat

It's no wonder that my Grandpa White told me, all those years ago, that Harold Morrill wore more hats than any man he'd ever known. The paper went on to list the various organizations he had been a part of, and then continued.

"He united with the Monson Baptist Church when he was a young man and for many years sang in the choir. He was a charter member of the

159

Monson band and until his railroad work took so much of his time he played baritone. In his town he was an energetic person, holding important town office for many years and serving on important committees from time to time. Many years ago he was elected to the board of trustees of Monson Academy and was president of the board and chairman of the executive committee at the time of his death. He was a member of the Monson Men's club.

On December 24th, 1885, Mr. Morrill was united in marriage to Miss Hattie Flint of Abbot who passed away on May 17th, 1939. By this union two daughters were born, Mrs. Beatrice Evans of Portland and Mrs. Ruth Campbell of Augusta.

Mr. Morrill was a man of sterling qualities, always busy but never too busy but what he could serve on various committees, especially of a civic nature. His interest in all things that pertained to the welfare of the citizens of his own town and community was unparalleled and marked him as a man of fine character, sound, dependable in his convictions, honest and true in his dealings with all mankind."

The Monson Railroad was one year-old when Harold Morrill went to work as a twenty-year old fireman in 1884. Fifty-four years later, in 1938 he retired. The railroad disbanded in 1943. Harold E. Morrill passed away in 1945.

During those fifty-four years, he was the heart and soul of the Monson Railroad, and a very important part of Monson Village.

The splash that he made in 1934, in a young boy's life, is still an influence in 1999, over sixty-five years later.

I've often wondered if it broke his heart when his railroad was no more.

ACKNOWLEDGEMENTS

I wish to thank Wayne and Estella Bennett, and Glenn Poole for their support in researching the Monson Historical Society Archives, and providing me with an index of articles about the Monson Railroad.

I wish to thank Karl and Edwina Kleeman for proof reading and fixing all my mistakes.

A special thank you to Vangi DeMaster for coaxing me out of my comfort zone and encouraging me to step in to community theater as an actor and director. I suppose I should thank her for proof reading as well, Thanks Vangi.

Of course, I want to thank my wife Roxanne for being my wife and best friend.

I also want to acknowledge the folks at the Thompson Free Library in Dover-Foxcroft, Maine, for their wonderfully maintained online archive library of the Piscataquis Observer newspaper. Without these articles this book would not have been possible.

All photos are courtesy of the Monson Historical Society except the photo's on Pages 3 and 122. Those photo's are of my Grandmother and Grandfather and my Father Billy and his brother Vernon, and are from the Author's collection.

All newspaper articles are from the Piscataquis Observer except as noted.

References

The Pullen Farm Revisited 1916-1937

Winston E. Pullen copyright 1996

Monson Village a History of Monson, Maine 1822-1997

Various Authors Printed by Kelly-Smith 1997

Two Foot to the Quarries The Monson Railroad

Robert C. Jones copyright 1998

Made in the USA
Columbia, SC
02 May 2021

36590294R00096